## "What did you t[hink you were] playing at in there?"

"I was playing at being your fiancé?" he replied.

"You overacted the part," Emma accused furiously.

"I thought I did rather well, considering the circumstances," Frazer replied stoically.

"Oh? And what about all those references to us sharing a bed, and that rubbish about my getting up at five to do the milking?"

"Well, he needed putting in his place. I'm sure you could get up at 5:00 a.m. if you wanted to." Frazer grinned. "And as for the references about us sharing a bed, I was just getting into character." Frazer's voice dropped to a low, intimate note. "And I wouldn't be happy about you getting out of it too early, either." He smiled as he noted the two high spots of color that burned on her cheeks now.

"A little bit of subtlety wouldn't have gone amiss." She tried not to be sidetracked.

"I don't think you have much leeway to preach about subtlety. You were the woman that dropped me into the damn situation in the first place."

**Kathryn Ross** was born in Zambia, where her parents happened to live at that time. Educated in Ireland and England, she now lives in a village near Blackpool, Lancashire. Kathryn is a professional beauty therapist, but writing is her first love. As a child she wrote adventure stories, and at thirteen was editor of her school magazine. Happily, ten writing years later, *Designed with Love* was accepted by Harlequin. A romantic Sagittarian, she loves traveling to exotic locations.

## About the author:

**Kathryn Ross** is a much-loved Harlequin Presents® author with a lively, intense, sophisticated writing style. She especially enjoys creating strong heroes and spirited heroines, and *Romantic Times* has praised the way Kathryn "utilizes dynamic characterization…to give the reader a gratifying reading experience." Her latest novel, *Terms of Engagement*, highlights this talent and we hope you'll enjoy this story as much as Kathryn enjoyed writing it!

# *Kathryn Ross*

## TERMS OF ENGAGEMENT

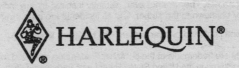

# HARLEQUIN®

TORONTO • NEW YORK • LONDON
AMSTERDAM • PARIS • SYDNEY • HAMBURG
STOCKHOLM • ATHENS • TOKYO • MILAN • MADRID
PRAGUE • WARSAW • BUDAPEST • AUCKLAND

ISBN 0-373-12204-7

TERMS OF ENGAGEMENT

First North American Publication 2001.

**Printed in U.S.A.**

# CHAPTER ONE

EMMA'S eyes widened at the breathtaking absurdity of her friend's suggestion. 'Jonathan and I had a civilised divorce, Tori, but it would still have to be a freezing day in hell before I'd ask him for help.'

'Well, it's nearly winter, and I believe it snows a lot in Scotland; you might not have long to wait,' Tori said brightly. 'Personally, I'd sell that place and get back down to London and civilisation quickly.'

'I don't want to come back to London. Of course I miss you, and my other friends, but the peace and tranquillity here are just what I needed.'

As if to prove the point to herself, Emma transferred the phone to her other hand and pulled back the curtain on the window next to her chair.

The sun was starting to go down. Golden light reflected on the smooth waters of the loch and bathed the mountains in a mellow, misty glow, highlighting the September colours of red and gold in the patchwork of fields. Swallows were flying low over the loch, wheeling and skimming after invisible prey. Soon they would leave for the winter, but she would stay, she vowed silently.

'So how is Jonathan?' she breathed in a soft undertone, dropping the curtain back into place.

'The same as ever, as far as I could tell. Mind you, I didn't stay at the party for very long. Jonathan was the guest of honour, and as you can imagine it was hard to get to speak to him. Word had just got out that he was about to start casting for his next big movie. Apparently it's a historical epic. People were all over him.'

Emma could just imagine. Jonathan liked to be the centre

of attention. He was a very successful film producer and he usually attracted a sycophantic crowd wherever he went.

'Anyway, we spoke briefly. He asked if I'd like a small part in his new movie and I told him I'd just landed the lead role in Tom Hubert's new film. That took the wind out of his arrogant sails.' Tori's laugh was the tinkling, attractive sound of pure pleasure.

'He's got good intentions, Tori,' Emma said, impulsively defending her ex-husband. 'Jonathan isn't all bad.'

'You know your problem, Emma? You're too nice. Jonathan walked out on you. In my eyes that makes him a rat of the first order,' Tori replied.

'It was a mutual decision. We both agreed it was best to go our separate ways,' Emma insisted firmly, then quickly moved on. 'So, what else did he say?' She didn't want to talk about her marriage break-up; even after two years it was still a raw subject.

'Just that he was looking for some wild and moody location for his film. Somewhere—and I quote—"atmospheric. A moor, a loch and an old baronial hall haunted with atmosphere."'

Emma's eyes widened. 'That's exactly how I described this place to you when we spoke on the phone last time.'

'I know. It was as if destiny had just intervened in your life.'

Emma smiled. Tori could be very dramatic, but then she was an actress.

'So I couldn't resist, Emma. I had to tell him all about your mysterious uncle who died and left you his estate in Scotland.'

'You didn't tell him he'd left me his debts and that the place was practically falling down around me, did you?'

'No, of course not. I told him his description matched the one you had given me of your property. That you had been living up there for a month and that you were in love with the place. I gushed positively over everything in your life, darling, I really did. You'd have loved it.'

Emma wasn't so sure about that. 'What was his reaction?' she asked cautiously.

'He'd already heard a rumour that you'd left London...' Tori hesitated. 'Actually he said, "I give her a month before she's running back to the city. She's the type to get withdrawal symptoms when she leaves the five-mile radius of the beauty counters at Knightsbridge."'

Emma's hands balled into tight fists at her side. How dared he say something so condescending? It just went to prove he had never really known her at all. She'd show him, she vowed silently.

'But he did also go on to say that he would be very interested to take a look at your estate. That it sounds a promising location for his purposes.'

'He can go to hell. He's not coming here.'

'Don't be hasty, Em. Do you know how much money they pay out for the right film location? It's not peanuts, I can assure you.'

'I know.'

'You did tell me you would do anything to be able to stay up there? But that the level of debt outstanding against the property is too much, not to mention the work that needs doing to the place?'

'Yes.' Emma's voice was flat.

'So this could be your chance to put things right. He's at the Hilton in London for two more nights, and he gave me his number. All you have to do is telephone him and tell him you're interested and he'll add your address to the list of properties his location manager will visit next week.'

Emma hesitated. 'I'll think about it.'

'Good. I've got to go, Emma. Speak to you soon.'

The silence in the room seemed overwhelming after the conversation.

Before the phone call she had been happily unpacking a

trunk full of her clothing and footwear. The cocktail dresses and smart business suits she had once needed for her job as PA to a high-flying television executive were spread incongruously about the small study. She needn't have bothered bringing them, because there was no way she would be wearing them again.

She glanced around the study. The faded heavy chintz curtains and the mismatched assortment of chairs had all seen better days. Yet there was an elegance to the room. It had dark panelled walls and a large inglenook fireplace which spoke of the grandeur of bygone days. Only a few rooms in the house were habitable. The floor in the east wing was rotted through with woodworm. Some of the upstairs bedrooms let in the rain because the roof leaked.

Just thinking about these problems brought a rush of panic about whether or not she had done the right thing, rushing up here from London. She had given up a perfectly good job. All right, she hadn't been earning fortunes, but at least she had been able to afford to run her flat. This estate was well out of her league.

Maybe ringing Jon was a good idea. Tori was right; they did pay big money for film locations—money she could use to transform this place.

If it was anyone else but her ex-husband she would be picking up the phone right now. But the thought of speaking to him, maybe seeing him again, made her blood pump through her veins like molten lava. It wasn't that she held any romantic ideas that she might still have feelings for him. Her love for Jon had died the day he'd walked out. She was more afraid of the fact that seeing him again would probably stir up painful memories, and she couldn't face that. She'd rather manage on her own.

Emma returned her attention to her clothes. Lifting up a black plastic bag, she started to throw some of the things in. Maybe she should ask Tori to sell them for her in

London. It was all designer gear and would fetch a good price.

Her hand paused over a pair of silver stilettos. Jon had bought them for her to attend the première of one of his films. There was a long silver dress that went with them.

She rooted through the clothes on the chair and found the dress, to hold it up against her slender figure. Then, on some wild impulse, she found herself kicking off her sturdy boots, jeans and jumper and slipping into the slinky dress. She stepped into the stilettos and walked across to the mirror on the wall.

Her reflection was a ghostly shimmer in the fading evening light. The dress was exquisite. It clung to her womanly curves, highlighting the firm swell of her breasts, the narrow waist. Her long, strawberry-blonde hair was wild about the pallor of her small face. She lifted it up, twisting it and tucking it into the sophisticated style she had worn that evening long ago, with Jon on her arm.

They had been a happy couple that night. But then that had been before they had started trying for a family, before they had found out that she could never bear him a child. When that knowledge had entered their relationship Jon's love for her had started to wither and die.

The light was fading fast, and she reached to switch on the lamp beside her. Golden light cheered the room for just a second, then went out. Frowning, she tried the overhead light. She flicked the switch several times but no light came on.

'Damn!' Her voice was unnaturally loud in the silence of the room. She would have to find some candles and go down and check out the fuse-box in the cellar. The thought made a shiver of unease rush through her.

Although she loved the solitude here during the day, at night the isolation was a bit intimidating. She certainly didn't want to be without electric light.

Emma went across to the bureau by the window and

rifled through the drawers until she found some matches. As she straightened a loud banging noise resounded through the house.

Emma dropped the box of matches on the floor in shock. It took her a moment to realise it was someone knocking forcefully against the front door.

Who on earth could that be? she wondered nervously. She was out in the middle of nowhere and she hadn't heard a car engine.

Retrieving the matches from the floor, she then tried to peek cautiously out of the window towards the door.

It was impossible to see who was standing there because of the awkward angle, and with the onset of darkness a mist was rolling in over the loch. It hung in heavy, damp swathes over the front gardens. There was an eeriness about the scene. She decided that she wouldn't answer the door. Again someone struck the knocker against the door. Whoever it was, they were very impatient.

She moved quietly out to the hallway, wondering if she could see whoever it was from the window there.

The letterbox rattled as someone lifted it. It made Emma's heart pound with apprehension.

'Mrs Sinclair?' a deep voice with a rolling Scottish accent asked. 'Mrs Sinclair, I'm Frazer McClarran, your next-door neighbour.'

The name was familiar. Her late uncle's solicitor had mentioned a Frazer McClarran. She racked her brain to remember what he had told her. It had been something to do with the fact that her uncle Ethan had had a long-running feud going with the man. She had no idea what it was about, but the memory was not reassuring.

'What do you want?' she called out cautiously, unwilling to open up the door to a total stranger.

'A member of your livestock has escaped, causing considerable damage on my property.' The voice held barely concealed impatience.

'How do you know it belongs to me?'

'Because there is a big red E branded on the creature's butt,' the voice grated. 'And if talk around the village is correct, that means it now belongs to you.'

Emma hesitated.

'Mrs Sinclair, are you going to open the door? Or should I just unload the animal onto your front porch? I can't hang around here all night; I've got things to be doing.'

'Hold on a moment.' There was an old oil lamp on the hall table. It took her a few moments to light it with the matches, and the glow did little to illuminate the vast hall-way, but it was better than nothing. She put the chain on the front door and swung it open a crack.

'Can you come a bit closer, please, so that I can see you?' she asked crisply.

'What are you doing? Checking I'm not an alien?' The voice held a hint of amusement now. It was an attractive voice—husky, sexy.

'How do I know that you are who you say you are?' she asked.

'Well, I haven't got a password, but I do have your damn goat in the back of my Land Rover.' He hesitated, then his voice softened. 'Look. I didn't mean to startle you. I'll tie the animal up out here and you can deal with it yourself when I'm gone.'

The gentle concern in the Celtic voice brought her senses rushing back. So, OK, her uncle had had a disagreement with his neighbour, but that didn't mean the guy was dangerous.

She closed the door, unhooked the chain and swung it open again.

Frazer McClarran's appearance was quite a revelation. He was about her age, thirty-two, and very good-looking if you went for the dark swarthy, rugged type. Which she didn't, she told herself firmly. She wasn't interested in getting involved with any man again.

He wore a crew-neck sweater. Its thick cream cable looked good against his dark skin. The black jeans hugged lithe hips and long legs.

The flickering light from her lamp played over his features, highlighting the glitter of black eyes, the powerful line of his shoulders, the square, firm jawline. His hair had a slight curl to it, an unruly thickness that was very attractive.

They stared at each other. For an instant she had the impression that he was as surprised by her as she was by him. Then she remembered why. The long dress she wore was hardly what you'd describe as casual attire. She must look as if she had just stepped out from a summer ball, not an old hall that was half falling down.

His gaze moved over her in one comprehensive sweep of an appraisal, making her feel very self-conscious. Her long strawberry-blonde hair was in need of a taming brush to bring it under control, the dress showed every curve of her slender figure, and on her feet she wore the frivolous pair of silver high heels.

His gaze returned to the lamp she held in her hand. 'Have I interrupted a seance, or do you always walk about dressed like that with the lights off?' he asked with some amusement.

'A seance!' Talk about being cut down to size. She had thought she looked attractive in the dress, like Claudia Schiffer, not an eccentric clairvoyant. 'I've got a problem with the electricity,' she answered stiffly. She couldn't think of an excuse for her clothes, she didn't know why she had put the dress on. It had been a moment's whim, she supposed. A nostalgic backward glance at the way her life used to be. Anyway, it was none of his business.

'Have you paid the bill?'

'The bill?'

'The electricity bill,' he said patiently.

'Of course I have.' She glared at him.

He grinned. 'So what do you want to do about your other problem?'

'What other problem?' she asked, captivated by the darkness of his eyes. Were they really so olive-black, or was it just a trick of the light?

'The problem of your goat.' He waved a hand behind him. 'I have the creature in the back of my Land Rover. It's probably eaten its way through the seats by now.'

'Oh, yes.' She pulled herself together. 'Step inside for a moment. I'll just put a jumper on, then I'll come and give you a hand.'

His gaze flicked again to her shoes. His lips curved in wry amusement. 'Sure,' he drawled sceptically.

She bit down on a terse reply. It was obvious that her neighbour thought she would be about as much help as a butterfly on a building site.

He looked around as he stepped inside. 'It's years since I stepped over Ethan's threshold,' he remarked dryly. 'I bet he's turning in his grave.'

'Why?' She paused with her hand on the door to the study.

He shrugged his shoulders in a dismissive gesture. 'Are you going to be long? I've got work to get back to.'

'No, I'll be a minute.' She opened the door into the study and put the lamp down on the sideboard. 'It's late to be going back to work, isn't it?' she asked, reaching for her sweater and pulling it over the silver dress.

'Working on a farm isn't like working in an office, you know,' he drawled. 'You can't tell your animals that you're clocking off at five-thirty.' There was that amusement in his tone again.

He watched as she pulled her hair out from beneath the sweater, then kicked off the high heels and stuck her feet into her boots. She probably made a curious spectacle—a long silver skirt with a woollen sweater and hiking boots—but she didn't care. 'Ready when you are,' she said brightly as she finished lacing her boots and threw her hair out of her eyes.

His gaze wandered around the room, taking in the cocktail dresses and smart suits that lay sprawled over the furniture. 'What were you doing? Having a fashion show?'

'I was unpacking.'

He bent and picked up a shoe from beside him. It had delicate lacy straps and a high platform sole. 'You're planning on going for long walks over the moors, I take it?' he grated sarcastically.

She tried very hard not to blush. 'Something like that.' She grabbed the shoe away from him and refused to allow herself to explain that she had been in the process of getting rid of this stuff. 'Shall we go?'

'After you.' He waved towards the door and watched as she struggled to take forceful strides in the tight skirt.

It was cold outside. A full moon sailed majestically from behind silver-edged clouds, reflecting on the still waters of the loch.

'Where are you parked?' she asked. 'I didn't hear the car engine.' She was struggling to keep up with his long stride.

'I couldn't drive up to the house because your gate was locked across the approach road.'

'Sorry.' Why was she apologising? she wondered. After all, she hadn't known he was coming. She wished to heaven he'd slow down. He must be well aware that she was practically running to keep up with him.

His Land Rover came into view as they rounded a corner, an old, rickety vehicle that looked as if it had been left over from World War II. It wasn't until they reached the gate that Emma realised she would have to climb over it.

Frazer hitched himself up over the five-bar gate with ease and swung his legs over to jump down the other side.

If she had been wearing her jeans it would have been no problem.

'Need a hand?' Frazer asked, one dark eyebrow raised as he turned to watch her.

'No, thanks. Just grab hold of the lamp.' She passed it over to him. He promptly took it, blew the flame out and put it down on the grass. 'We don't need it,' he said as she looked at him in some annoyance.

True enough, the night was bright. The moon had a powerful glow. It shone over the darkness of his hair, highlighting him like a charcoal drawing. Dark eyes, high cheekbones, his lips set in that almost arrogant firm slant, as if she was some insect who amused him.

She did the only thing she could do: hitched her dress up, giving a brazen glimpse of long shapely legs as she swung over to join him. She felt pleased that she had managed the manoeuvre with as much dignity as possible, then spoilt it by catching her foot awkwardly on the cattle-grid and stumbling.

Frazer reached out a hand, catching her around the waist and steadying her.

For a brief instant she was held very close to him, her body touching the long length of his. She could smell the aroma of soap from his jumper. It was fresh and clean and somehow warmly comforting.

Flustered, she pulled herself hastily away. 'Sorry.'

'That's OK.' He sounded matter-of-fact. Obviously her closeness hadn't had the same effect on him.

'Don't know how the goat got out.' She forced herself to talk in an effort to cover her awkwardness. 'There are cattle-grids on all the gates.'

'There are umpteen gaps in your hedges, your stone walls need maintenance and your fences are all a disgrace,' Frazer commented wryly. 'An elephant could get out.'

'Please feel free not to hold back on your criticism,' Emma muttered with sarcasm, her moment of awkwardness forgotten.

'I suppose it's your business if you want to let your livestock roam the country,' he replied tersely. 'But it does become mine when they wander onto my land and wreak havoc.'

'I'm sorry.' She had to admit he had a point. 'Did the goat do a lot of damage, then?'

He flicked a look at her as he went across to open the back of the Land Rover. 'If you call eating four pairs of underpants and some bedlinen a lot of damage.'

'Four pairs of...' She wanted to laugh suddenly.

He glanced at her again. She was very glad that the moon chose that moment to go behind a cloud. She shouldn't laugh. It was destruction of someone else's property. But she couldn't help being amused.

'Your wife must have been annoyed.' She kept a serious note in her voice with difficulty.

'I don't have a wife, just a housekeeper, and she was not best pleased.'

Emma went to stand next to him.

The goat stared at them both, its eyes reflecting brightly as the moon once more glided out from behind the clouds.

'Come on, you pest.' Frazer's voice was gentle as he reached for the rope he had tied around its neck.

The goat gave a baleful bleat. It sounded loud in the night air. 'Come on, now. I haven't all night.' Frazer leaned in so that he didn't have to drag the animal with unnecessary force. It bleated again, and backed away from him, its hooves making a scraping sound on the floor.

'Seeing as you're here, grab the end of the rope, will you?' Frazer muttered to Emma as he climbed into the back of the vehicle.

She noticed that his voice held a kinder, more patient note when he was talking to the animal than when he spoke to her.

He moved to pick the animal up, but missed as it made a dash for the door.

'Catch her—'

Too late, the animal shot past Emma. She caught hold of the end of the rope as it whipped by and then found herself running behind the animal over the uneven turf, unable to stop it.

'Let go, for heaven's sake, or you'll kill yourself.'

Instead she yanked at the rope, determined to get the animal to stop, turned over on her ankle, lost her balance and fell. She looked up in time to see the goat making a brave leap across a small mountain stream and disappearing through a hole in the hedge.

'Are you OK?' Frazer strolled over and offered her his hand.

Ignoring it, she got to her feet. 'I'm fine.' She brushed her hand over her clothes. Apart from the fact that there was a huge grass stain on the front of her silver dress, she was relatively unscathed.

'Let that be a lesson—don't attempt farming in your ball-gown,' Frazer murmured with a tinge of humour.

'Very funny.'

Frazer grinned. 'Well, I guess there's nothing more you can do about old nanny goat until the morning. I suggest you get one of your farm labourers to find her first thing. Don't leave her to wander.'

'Of course I won't,' Emma murmured. 'I'll get Brian onto it in the morning.' She picked some old twigs and pieces of bracken from the wool of her sweater.

'Brian Robinson? Is he still working here?' Frazer sounded incredulous.

'Yes. Why do you ask?'

Frazer shook his head and walked to close the back doors of his Land Rover. 'I suppose you are going to put this place up for sale?' he asked, ignoring her question.

'No. I'm planning on staying, making a success of it.'

'On your own?' He sounded shocked.

'Why not?'

Then he laughed.

Emma glared at him. Was he going to make bigoted remarks like Jon? 'What's so funny?' she asked tersely.

'No offence, but you don't look like the type to be stuck out here.' His voice was dry. 'Do you know anything about farming?'

'I'm learning.'

'Who's teaching you?'

'I've got books from the library—'

'You're not serious?' He laughed again.

'I've got the farm-hands, people who are experienced and trustworthy.' She was starting to lose her temper. He was dangerously close to sounding like her ex-husband.

'People like Brian?' His tone was sarcastic. 'Let me give you some advice. Don't trust him around your livestock unless he's well supervised.'

'I don't need any advice, thank you,' she said stiffly.

'Suit yourself.' He shrugged. 'When you get fed up playing farm, get in contact with me. I'd be interested in buying the place. I could use the extra land.'

'It's not for sale.'

'I'll offer you a good price.'

'It's not for sale,' Emma repeated firmly.

'Whatever you say.' He shrugged again, and glanced at his watch. 'Do you want me to walk with you back to the house? See if I can sort out your electrical problem before I go?'

Emma was sorely tempted to say yes, but that would be admitting she needed a man's help, and she wasn't about to do that. 'No, I'll manage. But thank you.'

He nodded. 'You know, you remind me a lot of your uncle Ethan,' he remarked.

With that he swung himself into the driver's seat of his Land Rover and started the engine.

'See you around,' he said, without glancing at her again.

Emma watched as he drove away. What had he meant by that crack about being like her uncle? she wondered. Men were the most irritating of creatures, she thought with exasperation.

# CHAPTER TWO

THE watery afternoon sunlight filtered through the damp haze hanging over the fields.

Highland cattle lifted their heads as Emma's small car disturbed the peaceful sound of the birds and the gurgle of the freshwater stream. They watched with curious eyes as she drove past them on the narrow road.

For once Emma didn't notice the magnificent animals; their shaggy coats and melting brown eyes were lost on her. Emma's eyes were firmly on the road, which twisted and turned through the mountain scenery, but her mind was on the phone call she had made last night.

What had possessed her? she asked herself, for what had to be the millionth time. After Frazer McClarran had left last night, she had been filled with a fighting spirit. She would show him that she was well able to cope up here, she had told herself firmly. And in that mood of determination she had fixed the problem with the electricity with surprising ease. Then, fired by her success and a feeling of confidence, she had picked up the phone and rung her ex-husband.

Tori was right. Why not use her contacts if it would help her to stay here? It didn't matter that her contact was Jonathan; their feelings for each other were in the past. They had both moved on now.

That bold spirit had been short-lived. Just hearing Jonathan's voice had set a lot of poignant emotions into play. She didn't love him, but she couldn't hate him either. He had sounded so happy...but then why wouldn't he be? Emma had seen pictures of his wife in a glossy magazine. Gina was incredibly beautiful...and they had a child now, something Jon had wanted above all else. Firmly Emma turned her thoughts away from that raw subject.

She wished her ex-husband well in his new life, but she didn't want to know about it. When he had informed her on the phone that he was accompanying his location manager up to Scotland, and that he would personally call and take a look at her property, she had been taken aback—and totally horrified. But it had been too late to back out by that point, so she had found herself offering to book some accommodation for them both at the local inn. They would arrive tomorrow afternoon.

Emma's hand tightened on the steering wheel. A feeling of ominous foreboding lay heavy in her heart.

She slowed her car as another vehicle came into sight. She recognised it as Frazer McClarran's Land Rover. He looked as if he was having problems because it was positioned off the road with the bonnet up. A smile curved Emma's lips. This might be fun.

She brought her car to a halt behind his and got out. 'Morning, Mr McClarran,' she said brightly.

Frazer stuck his head up from underneath the bonnet. 'Good morning.' His eyes moved over her slender figure. She was wearing faded jeans and a silky knit beige jumper which clung to her womanly curves. 'Almost didn't recognise you without your ballgown and boots.'

She hid her irritation behind a smile, and went to peer over his shoulder into the grimy depths of his engine. 'Having problems?' Her voice was light.

'No, I like standing here with my head under the bonnet of my car. It protects me from the fierce Scottish sun.' He flicked her an amused glance.

She smiled at him innocently, batting wide blue eyes, and then, pushing a well-manicured hand through the luxurious length of her hair, enquired, 'Can I be of some assistance?'

'I doubt it.' He grinned. 'Unless you carry a spanner in your handbag.'

'Sorry.' She smiled, as if unaware that he was being sarcastic. She watched for a moment as he tinkered about unsuccessfully.

He was wearing blue jeans teamed with a blue crew-neck jumper. His body was well toned, not an ounce of spare flesh on him, a hard, flat stomach, powerful shoulders. She wondered if he worked out.

'Don't let me detain you.' He glanced around at her again.

'That's OK. I'm not in a hurry.'

She watched for a little while longer, then suggested softly, 'Maybe you've got some dirt in the carburettor?'

'I don't think so.'

'Have you checked it?'

He glared at her.

She ignored the look and smiled provocatively. 'Or perhaps it's just a loose connection?'

'Look, I suggest you get off to do your shopping,' he muttered. 'And leave me to fix my car in peace.'

'If you want.' Then with another smile she reached into the engine. 'I'll just have a look before I go.'

Frazer stood back, staring at the back of her red-gold head with barely concealed impatience. He could smell her perfume, a flowery, feminine scent, not unappealing. Then his eyes moved to the shapely line of her bottom in those jeans. 'Look, Mrs Sinclair, do you mind getting out of my way?' he grated.

'Fine.' She straightened and bent to wipe her hands on the damp grass verge. 'I'll think you'll find that it's all right now,' she said with quiet confidence.

'What do you mean?' He stared at her as if she had suddenly grown another head.

'I mean if you try the engine it should start.' She smiled. 'That is unless you really like standing with your head under the bonnet, sheltering from the fierce Scottish sun?' She couldn't resist the jibe, before sauntering back to her own car.

Frazer McClarran got back into his vehicle and tried the engine. It fired into life with the first turn of the ignition key. The look of astonishment on his face as she drove past him made Emma chuckle to herself all the way down the steep mountain roads.

The small village of Glenmarrin lay on the coast, a few miles away from Emma's land. It was a picturesque fishing port which nestled in the curve of the bay, surrounded by the majesty of the mountainous countryside. It had one main street, with a few shops and houses around the harbour, and was the sort of place where everyone seemed to know everyone else.

Emma parked her car by the harbour and walked across the road to pick up some groceries at the small supermarket. The first day that Emma had ventured down here for supplies she had found herself the centre of attention. Everyone had seemed very friendly.

Mrs Murray, the proprietor of the shop, greeted Emma warmly now as she walked through the door. She was a cheery woman, large and attractive, with a laugh that was infectious.

'How are you settling in, dear?' she asked politely as she rang up Emma's purchases on the till.

'Very well, thank you.'

'If you have any problems, you can always ask your neighbour, you know—Frazer McClarran. Lovely man.'

'Yes, we have met. He seems nice enough,' Emma replied nonchalantly.

'Nice?' The woman looked at her with a raised eyebrow. 'There are men and then there are *men*. Frazer McClarran is in a league of his own—a tower of strength to the community. A member of the mountain rescue team, a hard worker, a loyal friend.'

Emma felt as if she was being reprimanded. 'I'm sure he is.'

'He's also a confirmed bachelor. Every eligible woman in the town has made a play for Frazer, but he's not one to be tied down.'

'Maybe he just hasn't met the right woman.'

Emma smiled to herself as she walked back to her car to put her provisions in the boot. Frazer might be a member of the mountain rescue team, but she had done the rescuing today.

The sun had taken possession of a suddenly bold blue sky. All that remained for Emma to do was go into the Traveller's Rest Hotel and book her ex-husband a room.

The knowledge dulled her amusement and brought back her earlier uncertainties. Her instincts told her this wasn't a good idea. Indeed, it could be a vast mistake.

Emma's eyes moved to the old black and white building further up the road, the only hotel in the area. Her steps were slow as she headed back towards it. A seagull on the roof watched her approach, then seemed to let out a wild, cackling laugh. Maybe he agreed with her, Emma thought wryly. She had probably taken leave of her senses. But then desperate situations called for desperate measures.

As she crossed the road, a sudden flurry of rain started. It was so totally unexpected that it made her gasp. Her head down against the cold downpour, she ran the last few yards to the steps of the hotel. Her long hair obscuring her vision, she didn't see the man who was also running towards the steps from the opposite direction. They collided with a jolt.

'I'm sorry.' He reached out a hand to steady her.

She looked up, and found herself looking into Frazer McClarran's dark eyes.

'It's you again,' she murmured breathlessly.

The rain was cool against her skin. It trickled over the thickness of her eyelashes, blurring his handsome features for a moment.

'Better get in out of this,' he said. His hand still resting at her waist, he ushered her politely up and through the doors.

'Whew! I wasn't prepared for that,' she said, brushing the rain off her face and running a smoothing hand over her hair. 'I thought it was going to be sunny this afternoon.'

'Always expect the unexpected in Glenmarrin,' he said with a wry grin. 'Maybe I should have remembered that myself, when I ran into you this morning.'

She grinned back at him. 'How is the car?'

'Fine, thanks.' His eyes flicked briefly over her appearance. She was wet, and the pale ribbed jumper clung tightly over a very shapely outline. 'Where did you learn to fix a car like that?'

'I have two brothers who are both car-mad.' She was trying not to notice the way he had just looked at her. Was it her imagination or had there been a glimmer of male interest in those dark eyes? 'I decided to beat them at their own game and did a course at college on car maintenance a few years ago.'

'Very impressive.'

'It put you in your place anyway.' She smiled.

He had the grace to cringe. 'I'm sorry. Was I being patronising?'

'Just a little.'

'I was having a bad morning.' He smiled. 'I hope you won't hold it against me.'

Heavens, when he smiled at her like that she would let him get away with almost anything, she thought. Frazer McClarran was gorgeous. The notion discomfited her. He wasn't her type, she told herself firmly. He was off-limits. She had given men up.

'So what are you doing here?' he asked casually.

'I want to book a couple of rooms for…some friends.' She faltered slightly, wondering if she should say it was for her ex-husband, then decided forcefully that was her own business. 'What about you?'

'I'm organising a stag night here tomorrow night.'

'Oh?' Was he getting married? she wondered. Maybe Mrs Murray didn't know everything.

'Did you get your errant goat back under lock and key?'

'Yes, your underwear is safe again.' She smiled, a mischievous glint in her eyes. 'Molly is back where she belongs. But it took three of us this morning to catch her.'

He laughed. 'Rosa will be pleased.'

'Rosa?'

'My housekeeper.'

They were interrupted by a woman coming out to the reception desk beside them. She was an attractive blonde in her early twenties. 'Frazer, this is a nice surprise,' she said cheerfully. 'What brings you in here on a Friday afternoon?'

'Mark's stag night.' Frazer turned with a smile. 'How are you, Angela?'

It wasn't his stag night, Emma noted. Not that it made a blind bit of difference to her whether this man was about to be married or not.

'Bearing up, under the circumstances.' Angela patted her stomach. She wore a black dress that did little to disguise the fact that she was heavily pregnant.

'How long have you got to go now?'

'Another month, would you believe?'

'You're looking well.'

Angela laughed, then looked curiously at Emma.

'This is Emma Sinclair. Ethan Daniels' niece.'

'Pleased to meet you.'

Emma wondered if she was imagining the momentary look of surprise on the woman's face. It was as if she'd done a double take on her appearance.

'We were very sorry to hear about your uncle's death.'

'Thank you,' Emma said politely, then felt impelled to explain, 'I didn't really know him very well.'

'Not a lot of people did. He withdrew into himself after his daughter's death. Became a near recluse.'

There was a feeling of awkwardness for a moment. Then Angela said in a bright, businesslike tone, 'Well, Frazer, what can I do for you?'

'Better see to Mrs Sinclair first,' Frazer replied. 'She wants to book some rooms.'

'No, it's OK. You go ahead.' Emma was happy to put off the moment. She was starting to think she should ring Jon and tell him there was no accommodation available. 'I'm not in a hurry. I don't particularly want to go back outside until it stops raining anyway.'

Frazer shrugged. 'Fair enough. It's just that Mark's decided we should have the meal earlier, Angela, and there are a few extra guests now.'

As Emma listened idly her eyes moved over Frazer's long, lean form. She wasn't surprised to learn he was a member of the mountain rescue team. He was the epitome of the outdoor athletic type, ruggedly masculine, laden with sex appeal, yet so casually natural that he seemed totally unaware of it.

Emma's attention wandered. Her eyes moved over the reception area—a red tartan carpet and walls panelled with dark wood. The building was obviously hundreds of years old; the floors seemed to be uneven and the doorways through to the bar were low, the ceiling beamed with black oak. Through the open door she could see there was only one old man in the bar lounge. He was sitting by a large inglenook fireplace which held the remaining glimmer of a dying fire, a pint in front of him. He looked as if he was asleep.

She wondered what Jon would think of this place. His world was cocooned in absolute luxury; he only stayed in top-class hotels. She pulled herself up sharply. She didn't care what Jon thought. All she wanted was the opportunity to start her life afresh here.

'How many rooms did you want to book, Mrs Sinclair?' Angela finished dealing with Frazer and turned to her.

'Two singles for tomorrow night.' Emma was very conscious of the fact that even though Frazer's business was concluded he continued to stand next to her.

Angela turned on a computer screen next to her. 'Was it just for one night?'

'Yes, I think so.' She hoped so.

'And what name is the booking to be made in?'

'Lesley May and Jonathan Sinclair.' Emma felt very uncomfortable now. The woman keyed in the names and smiled at her.

'They're flying up from London to Edinburgh in the morning, then driving here. They should arrive late in the afternoon.'

'That's fine,' Angela said easily.

'Thank you.' Emma swallowed hard. There, she'd done it.

She'd face Jon tomorrow and pretend to herself that he was just a stranger.

She turned and looked up at Frazer. For a fleeting second he noticed the haunting sadness in her eyes. Then she smiled, and the shadows were banished, making him wonder if he had imagined them.

'It's still raining,' he remarked, looking towards the doors. 'I'm going to have a coffee in the lounge. Would you care to join me?'

Emma hesitated, then nodded. Company was just what she needed to take her mind off what she had just done. 'That would be lovely, thank you.'

'I'll get Sandra to bring them through for you,' Angela said as they made their way into the other room.

She noticed how Frazer had to bend his head to get into

the bar. The man by the fire looked up, then seemed to fall back to sleep again.

'Lively place, isn't it?' Frazer remarked with a grin as he led the way up to the sofas in the window. Emma sat opposite to him.

There was a feeling of tension as she met his eyes. It was strange, but he made her very aware of herself as a woman. She wondered if her hair was a mess after that rain, and wished now she had excused herself and gone to the ladies' before following him in here. The opportunity to refresh her lipstick and tidy her hair would have been most welcome. She moistened her lips nervously. His eyes rested for a moment on the softness of her mouth. There was something blatantly sensual about that look, something that made Emma's pulses quicken.

She searched for something to say, something to break the bizarre intimacy of the moment. 'When does your friend get married?' It was the best subject she could come up with.

'Saturday week.'

'It's to be hoped the weather picks up,' she said idly, looking past him at the rain which pounded against the windows, obscuring the view of the harbour in a watery haze.

'Yes, I hope so. Especially as they've hired a marquee for the occasion.'

'Apparently they come with heating installed, and it doesn't really matter if the weather isn't good,' she continued lightly.

'As long as it isn't blowing a gale,' Frazer said with a grin, 'they should be all right.'

When he smiled it lit his eyes. They were wonderfully warm and dark. With difficulty she turned her attention away from his good looks.

'Are you the best man?'

Frazer nodded. 'I've known Mark and Ruth for years.'

A young woman brought a tray of coffee and put it down on the table. She smiled at Frazer shyly, and blushed when he smiled back at her.

'Thanks, Sandra.'

She nodded and left them.

'That's Angela's young sister. She's seventeen.' Frazer reached to pour their drinks. 'Do you take cream and sugar?' He glanced up at her.

'No, I take it black, thanks.'

'So where do you hail from, Emma? May I call you Emma?' he asked casually.

'Please do.' She noticed how small the delicate cup and saucer looked in his hand. She took the drink from him, being careful not to brush against his skin. Why, she couldn't have said.

This man was having a very curious effect on her.

Emma leaned back in the sofa and crossed her long legs, trying her best to appear relaxed. 'I was brought up in Kent, but I've lived most of my life in London.'

'So you're a country girl at heart?'

She smiled. 'I like to think so, but I've still got a lot to learn.'

'You're determinedly forging your way through those library books?' He laughed.

She felt herself colouring with embarrassment. 'I know it probably sounds silly to you. Obviously there is no sub-stitute for experience. But I've got to start somewhere.'

He nodded. 'It doesn't sound silly. I shouldn't have laughed,' he said gently.

The sincere note in his voice made her senses respond to him in a very strange manner. Maybe her first judgement of him had been harsh.

'I was just stunned that you were attempting to run that estate on your own with no real knowledge of even the basics of farming.'

'I'm getting the hang of things,' she assured him swiftly. 'And I've got farm labourers to help.'

'You've got guts. I'll give you that.' He leaned forward, an earnest light in the darkness of his eyes. 'But you know that estate is in a bad state of disrepair. It's going to be bleak there this winter. Life can be harsh up here at the best of times.'

She felt the hand of reality settle firmly on her shoulder, and with it disappointment. 'This isn't a prelude to you offering to buy the estate from me again, is it?' she asked warily. 'Because, if so, the answer is still no.'

'It's just neighbourly concern,' he said gently. 'Ethan's estate isn't really the place for a young widow on her own. Especially a woman who is used to the city.'

'Well, I can assure you I'm going to be fine,' Emma said firmly. 'And I'm not a widow,' she corrected him. 'I'm divorced.'

'Oh!' He sat back. 'I'm sorry. The talk in the village was that you were recently widowed.'

Emma's eyes widened. 'I don't know where they got that idea from.'

He laughed. 'Did you ever play that game Chinese Whispers when you were a child?'

She smiled. 'Yes, I think I did.'

'Well, Glenmarrin is the home of that kind of gossip. What one person says is distorted as it passes down the chain, until it bears little resemblance to the truth once it reaches the last person in the line. And the trouble is you can't avoid hearing the rumours even if you try. News of a young widow inheriting Ethan's place has been the number one subject for weeks.'

'Sounds like the social scene in London. Maybe things in the country aren't so different after all.' Emma grinned, then added impulsively, 'Anyway, they'll probably all know the truth by tomorrow. I'm divorced, and one of the rooms I've just booked was for my ex-husband.'

Frazer studied her over the rim of his coffee cup. 'Are you planning on getting back together, then?'

'Heavens, no! He's just coming up to discuss some business. He's remarried now, to a very beautiful Italian girl called Gina.'

'But you've still got a soft spot for him?' Frazer hazarded a guess.

'No!' Emma's voice was emphatic, and louder than she had intended.

The man by the fire looked over at them curiously.

'Certainly not,' she repeated in a softer tone. 'Jon is a film producer and he's looking for a Scottish location for his latest production. He's going to take a look at my estate.'

Frazer made no reply to that, just continued to look at her with those intense dark eyes. There was something about those eyes that made her feel he could look into her soul. It unnerved her for a minute.

'They pay a lot of money for a good location,' she continued briskly. 'And, as you said yourself, the farm is very run down. I could do with an injection of cash.'

Frazer considered what she had told him for a moment, before saying calmly, 'It's none of my business, but it sounds to me like you're playing with fire.'

'What makes you say that?' Emma was instantly on the defensive.

He shrugged. 'Intuition.'

Emma didn't like the analysis, especially as it wasn't a million miles away from her own feelings, but out loud she said firmly, 'It just makes good business sense. Jon and I are still friends. What was between us is in the past.'

'As I said, it's none of my business anyway.' Frazer shrugged. 'What would I know? I've never been married.' He hesitated for a moment. 'I have learned though, that sometimes it's safer to leave the past behind you. Digging around in it can be a painful experience.' He finished his coffee and looked out towards the window. 'Sun is out.'

'So it is.' Emma wished it would rain again. She would have liked to ask him what had happened for him to draw that conclusion.

'If you change your mind about selling, give me a ring.' He got out his wallet to pay for their drinks and slid a card with his number on it towards her.

'I've already made it clear that I won't.'

'I'd be prepared to rent some of your lower pastures.' He smiled, not one bit deterred by her obstinacy. 'I'll pay good money. Maybe not as good as your film producer, but it's an option if you decide you don't want a lot of strangers trudging around your house.'

Emma picked up the card and played with it absently in her long fingers. 'I'll think about it.'

He nodded, and then glanced at his watch. 'I'd better get going. I've got a lot of work still to get through.'

'Yes, I have too.' Emma wondered if his earlier gentle friendliness had just been a ploy to soften her, so that he could get his hands on some of her land. She was surprised by how disappointed that idea made her feel.

Despite his words, he made no move to leave. Their eyes met. She felt a flare of red-hot heat inside her. Frazer McClarran was just too disturbingly sexy. Suddenly she found herself wanting to detain him, to talk to him some more.

'Can I ask you something?' she said impulsively.

'Sounds ominous.' He smiled.

Emma had never met a man whose smile could arouse butterfly sensations in her stomach. With determination she pushed the feelings away. 'I'm just curious to know why my uncle fell out with you.'

'Ah.' Frazer's lips twisted ruefully. 'It was an old feud between him and my father. So long ago now that I've almost forgotten what it was about. But Ethan didn't forget. He kept the fires well stoked even after my father died.'

'And you can't remember what it was about?'

Frazer shrugged. 'Ethan withdrew away from society after his daughter died. He was a very bitter, stubborn man. The more people tried to help him the more he drove them away.'

'I take it he wouldn't sell to you either,' Emma said with an impish grin.

'Something like that,' Frazer agreed. 'I told you. You're a lot like him.'

'Well, I wouldn't know. I never met my uncle, or for that matter my cousin who died.'

Frazer looked surprised. 'Why not?'

'It's a long story,' Emma said softly. 'And I wouldn't want to bore you with it.'

'I wouldn't be bored.' Frazer seemed to settle himself back down against the sofa.

'I suppose you knew Ethan and his family quite well? You sound as if you've lived in these parts for a long time.'

'My family go back several generations here.' Frazer nodded.

'Well…Ethan's brother, Robert, was my father. My mother met him when they were both studying at Oxford. Their affair was passionate and my mother fell wildly in love. But the relationship was never meant to be long-term as far as Robert Daniels was concerned. He had no intention of marrying my mother. In fact, when he discovered she was pregnant he said he didn't want to see her again. She left Oxford and went to live with her sister in Kent. My father got his degree and went back to take over the running of his family estate. I never met him.'

'A nice guy,' Frazer murmured caustically.

'Was he?' Emma asked, curious to hear any snippets of information about the man she had always wondered about.

'I was being facetious.'

Seeing the look of disappointment in her eyes, he added, 'To be honest, I don't remember him that well. He was Ethan's older brother, and the estate went to him after their father died. Then Robert died...I must have been about eleven at the time. If I remember correctly, it was a drowning accident.'

Emma nodded. 'Yes, it was. The only reason I know was that Ethan wrote to my mother and told her. Apparently, every year on my birthday my mother had sent my photograph to my father. I think she hoped for a long time that he would come after her and change his mind. But of course he never did. Never so much as wrote to acknowledge receiving the photographs. When Ethan inherited the estate after his death, he found the photographs bundled together at the bottom of a drawer.'

'But Ethan didn't invite you up to Scotland?' Frazer asked.

'No. After my father's death it was as if a curtain had been pulled down over the past. My mother married Tony and had two sons.'

'The car enthusiasts?'

Emma nodded. 'Sean is nineteen. He's off seeing the world. Taylor is twenty, married with a young baby. He's a rally driver, based in France at the moment.'

'And you've ended up inheriting your father's estate after all,' Frazer remarked.

'Ironic, isn't it?' Emma said lightly. 'Apparently I was Ethan's only living relative, so he made his will out to me. You can imagine my surprise when his solicitor tracked me down and his letter fell through my letterbox. I mean, I had never so much as received a Christmas card from my father or his brother. Then suddenly all their worldly possessions fell at my feet.' She was silent for a moment. 'I suppose it would have gone to Ethan's daughter had she lived.'

'I guess so,' Frazer agreed quietly. 'And maybe Ethan

felt guilty about the way his brother had treated your mother.'

Emma shrugged. 'I suppose I'll never know what he thought. I would have liked to have known him though…and my cousin, Roberta.' She smiled sadly for a moment. 'I once asked my mother for their address. I was only about fifteen at the time, and I had this romantic notion that I could turn up on their doorstep and be welcomed. She refused to give it to me and my stepfather was furious that I had asked…' She trailed off. What she didn't tell Frazer was that she had been very unhappy at that time in her life. She had never felt as if she'd fitted in to her mother's new life.

Frazer's eyes moved absently over her red-gold hair. 'You look like your cousin. Roberta had the same colouring, the same way of holding a man's attention.'

Emma didn't know how to take that remark. Was it a compliment? 'How well did you know her?'

'Fairly well. We were at school together for a while.' He hesitated. 'She was only twenty-five when she died.'

'So I heard. It was really very sad. No wonder Ethan felt bitter.'

Frazer inclined his head. 'I suppose you're right.' He glanced again at his watch. 'I've really got to go.'

'OK. Thank you for the coffee.' She wondered if she had talked too much. She didn't usually open up like that, especially to someone she hardly knew.

He looked over at her, held her eyes for a moment. 'Would you like to have dinner with me one night?' he asked suddenly.

The invitation made her blood rush like fire through her veins. She hesitated, then smiled and managed to say casually, 'That would be nice.'

He stood up. 'OK, I'll give you a ring and we'll arrange something.'

'It might be better to wait until after this weekend. I'll be fairly tied up with my ex-husband being here.'

'Fine.' He nodded towards the card that she still held in her hand. 'Meanwhile, think about my offer.'

Was that why he had asked her out? she wondered as she watched him walking away from her across the deserted bar. Or was she just being cynical?

She wondered if she had made a mistake accepting his invitation. Then she shrugged to herself. She was only thirty-two—too young to lock herself away in a convent. She could have fun, just as long as she didn't allow herself to get serious.

Trouble was, Frazer McClarran was seriously attractive.

# CHAPTER THREE

JON phoned as soon as he arrived in the village and suggested that Emma meet him for a drink that evening. He needed instructions on how to get to her property. Also, he wanted to discuss his requirements for filming.

So it was that Emma found herself strolling into the Traveller's Rest again the next evening. It was a wet September night, and Emma wished she had worn trousers. Not only was she cold, but the long floral skirt and black cashmere jumper suddenly didn't feel casual enough. She didn't want Jon to think she had made any kind of effort to impress him.

She put her umbrella in the stand by the door and peered into the bar. Unlike yesterday afternoon, when she had sat in there with Frazer, the room was packed. There was a huge log fire blazing in the stone fireplace and a smell of pine smoke mingled with the smell of malt whisky.

Her eyes flicked with apprehension over the crowd. She didn't see Jon, but she did see Frazer McClarran. He was standing in the doorway of what was probably the private function room, judging by the thumping music coming from it.

It was his friend's stag night this evening, she remembered.

He wore a dark suit and a blue shirt open at the neck. He looked fabulous. There was no other word to describe him. He glanced across, met her eyes and smiled. She felt her heart jolt against her chest as if a burst of electricity had shot through her.

'Emma.' A voice distracted her. 'Emma, over here.'

38

She looked over towards the corner of the room. Jon was sitting at a table by himself.

He stood up as she made her way across towards him. It was nearly two years since she had last seen her ex-husband, but he didn't seem to have changed. He was thirty-six now, yet he had the same blond smooth good looks, the same trendy way of dressing, as if he had just come off a Milan catwalk.

'Hello, Emma,' he said, a husky note in his voice.

She felt herself stiffen awkwardly as he reached to kiss her on the cheek.

He didn't seem to notice, just smiled at her. His hand rested a moment too long at her waist.

'Hello, Jon.' She stepped back from him. 'Where is your colleague?'

'Lesley won't be joining me until tomorrow.' He pulled out a chair for her.

'I see.' Emma was disappointed, she had been hoping there would be a third person present. It would have kept things more firmly on a business footing.

'Can I get you a drink?' he asked politely.

'Just an orange juice, thanks. I can't stay long.'

He frowned. 'I was hoping you might join me for some supper. I haven't eaten yet, and you know how I hate to eat alone.'

Yes, she did. She knew so much about him, she thought suddenly, her eyes moving over the firm contours of his face, the deep ocean-blue of his eyes. You didn't share four years of your life with someone without getting to know all the little things about them. Their pet hates, their passions.

'I can't, Jon. I'm sorry. I've already eaten.' That was a lie. She hadn't been able to face any food tonight because she had been so uptight before she came out. But she wouldn't spend any more time with Jon than was absolutely necessary.

'I see.' He sounded disappointed. 'I'll get you that drink, then.'

She watched as he walked to the bar. Then her eyes moved back to the doorway where Frazer had been standing a few moments ago. He had gone. Returned to the party, presumably. The door was closed and the muffled music that filtered through sounded like the kind played when someone was stripping. As it was a stag night, she supposed whatever was going on was typically raucous.

She imagined Frazer leaning against a bar watching some glamorous, curvaceous woman as she peeled off her clothing. For some reason the picture this conjured up was intensely unsettling.

Jon returned with their drinks. 'So how have you been?' he asked, taking the seat opposite.

'Fine. And you?'

'Great.' He paused. 'I was really stunned when I heard you'd moved up here, Emma. Whatever possessed you to bury yourself in a place like this?'

'I'm really happy here, Jon.'

He didn't look convinced.

'I believe congratulations are in order for you and Gina,' she continued, her manner brisk. 'I heard that you've become a father since I last saw you.'

'Yes.' He smiled and took out his wallet, flipping it open to slide a photograph towards her.

She looked at the cute baby, all smiles and dimples, and a part of her heart contracted with pain and regret. 'She's beautiful,' she said honestly. 'I'm happy for you.'

'Yes, she's the light of my life,' Jon said simply. 'We called her Bethany. She'll be one next week.'

Emma smiled and slid the photograph back to him. 'And how is Gina?' she asked politely.

'She's left me. Our divorce is just about finalised.'

The stark words made Emma sit back in shock. 'I didn't know.'

'She has custody of Bethany, but I'll have access. We're just working out the details.'

'I'm so sorry,' Emma said softly.

He shrugged. 'In many ways I suppose we weren't compatible. Not like you and I.' Jon's voice had taken on that husky quality she remembered so well, and his eyes were gentle on her face. 'I've been thinking about you a lot recently, Emma, thinking about what I lost when we parted.'

Alarm bells started to ring inside her. She didn't know what she had expected to happen when she saw her ex-husband again. She had been prepared to feel pain, regret, maybe, but she had never imagined for one moment he would get sentimental.

'Jon, I'm a different person now.' Swiftly, she changed the subject. 'So, about the location for your film. I took the liberty of bringing a few photographs of my house.'

Before she could pick up her bag to find them, he waved the idea aside. 'There's no point in my looking through them now. I'll come out tomorrow and see the place for myself, take a few of my own photographs with a wide-angle lens.'

He regarded her steadily over his glass of whisky. 'Strange how fate has brought us together again. If I hadn't bumped into your old friend Tori I might never have found your hiding place.'

'I'm not hiding myself away, Jon.' She frowned. 'What a strange thing to say.'

'Is it?' His blue eyes were piercing in their intensity. 'I've missed you, Emma. I can't tell you how much.'

The gently spoken words made her heart contract painfully.

'Stay and have supper with me, Em.' He leaned across the table earnestly.

'I'm sorry, I can't—'

'I know I hurt you in the past,' he interrupted her swiftly. 'And I want you to know how sorry I am.'

'There's no need for you to say that, Jon. You were honest with me. You...you wanted a family, and I don't blame you for that.' Her voice was little more than a whisper. 'There was no point in us living a lie.'

'Except that I feel as if I'm living a lie now, without you,' he murmured gently.

'It's too late for this, Jon.' She cut across him, her emotions in chaos. His arrogant assumption that she was pining away up here and would easily fall into his arms again offended her. Did he think she was so easy that all he had to do was murmur a few words of regret and she would be his again?

She looked into the deep blue of his eyes. She had loved him, given her heart totally to him. Maybe a part of her had hoped for a while that he would come back to her. But Jon had wanted a family more than he'd wanted a wife. They had sat down quite rationally and discussed the options: fostering, adoption. Jon hadn't been interested in any of those. It wouldn't be his own flesh and blood, he had said. So Emma had let him go. What else could she have done?

It hadn't taken him long to find a new partner, someone who had given him the child he wanted. That had hurt.

Did he think she had been sitting around here waiting for him, her life empty without him? Her eyes narrowed on the handsome features as anger came to her rescue. She had far too much pride to let him think for one moment that her life was empty without him.

'I think maybe you've had a couple of whiskys too many.' Before he could dispute this, she continued firmly, 'I asked you up here for a business reason, that's all. Besides, there is someone very special in my life now.' She threw the little white lie in for good measure, hoping it would make him keep his distance.

'Tori didn't tell me.' He looked stunned. 'Is it serious?'

'Yes.'

'I see.' He was quiet. 'I've made a fool of myself, haven't I?'

'No, of course not.' She felt wretched now. 'Look, let's just forget this conversation and talk about the film you're making. That's why you asked me to meet you tonight after all.'

He didn't answer her. He seemed shellshocked by her news.

'Are you going to marry him?' he asked, ignoring her entreaty.

She hesitated, wondering how far she should take this. Maybe she should say no. But then she might have to weather more talk about the past. 'Yes, I'm going to marry him,' she said finally.

Jon's eyebrow's rose. 'What's his name?'

'Frazer.' The name spilled automatically from her lips.

'I hope you know what you're doing,' Jon said tersely. 'You can't have known him long. You've only been in Scotland a little over a month.'

'Of course I know what I'm doing.' Her voice faltered. Did she know what she was doing? She wasn't a liar. She was a straightforward, honest person. This was wrong. Using Frazer's name was wrong. But then, no one would ever know, she told herself firmly, and Jon would be gone soon. 'It's a secret at the moment,' she found herself continuing. 'We don't want anyone to know until we've broken the news to his family. So I'd appreciate it if you didn't say anything to anyone.'

Jon shrugged. 'So where is he tonight?'

'At a stag night.' Emma's voice was hollow. Her daring mood had evaporated, leaving a feeling of trepidation in its wake.

'Not for your wedding!' He sounded horrified.

'No, someone else's wedding,' Emma replied calmly. 'Do you think we could get down to discussing business now?' she asked lightly.

'I suppose so.' Jon shrugged. He bent to pick up a brief-case that was sitting next to his feet. 'I've got a few of the requirements here—sizes of rooms, etcetera.'

She watched with a feeling of relief as he took out some printed sheets. The emotion was short-lived, however, because as she glanced up she saw Frazer heading across the room in their direction.

'Hi.' He stopped by their table and smiled, that lazy, attractive smile of his. 'How's it going?'

'Fine.' Her voice felt weak.

Frazer looked over at Jon. 'You must be Emma's ex-husband,' he said easily, holding out a hand. 'I'm Frazer McClarran. Emma's next-door neighbour.'

Jon was clearly taken aback. Emma could see that he was weighing Frazer up.

Emma debated saying something like, Oh, this isn't the Frazer that I've been telling you about. Backtracking quickly seemed the only option.

'And a bit more than that, from what I've been hearing.' Jon preempted her and stood up politely to shake Frazer's hand. 'Congratulations.'

Frazer looked puzzled, and Emma felt as if she desperately wanted someone to beam her up out of here. She opened her mouth to say something that would extricate herself from the embarrassing situation. No sound came out.

'I thought you were at a stag night?' Jon continued, his tone jovial.

'I am.' Frazer nodded towards the other room. 'I'm just taking a breather. I'm supposed to be minding the groom, so I won't intrude on you any longer.'

Maybe she was going to get away with this, Emma thought hopefully. If Frazer just left now it would be perfect.

'Don't rush off,' Jon said pleasantly. 'Let me buy you a drink.'

'No, really—'

'I insist.' Jon pulled out a spare chair. 'What will you have?'

Frazer hesitated, then sat down. 'OK. That's very kind of you. I'll have a Coke.'

'A Coke?' Jon's eyebrows rose. 'Won't you have something a bit stronger by way of a celebration drink?'

'No, Coke will be fine. I'm driving tonight.'

Frazer watched Jon as he walked away from them to the bar. 'I thought I'd made it clear that it wasn't my stag party. What is he talking about?'

Emma didn't answer him. Her heart was hammering fiercely against her chest.

'Emma?' He looked at her, noting the high colour in her cheeks. 'Do you know what he means? Why is he buying me a celebratory drink?'

Emma shrugged. 'He might somehow have got the impression that...that you and I are engaged,' she murmured, in a low, helpless tone.

'What?' Frazer stared at her. 'How the hell did he get that idea?'

She shrugged again. 'I...I might have given it to him,' she admitted.

He looked incredulous. Then annoyed. 'Why would you do that? We hardly know each other, for heaven's sake.'

'It was a mad, impulsive moment... I needed him to think I was involved with someone and you were the first available name that sprang to my lips.'

'Thanks!' Frazer raked a hand through the darkness of his hair. 'I know I asked you to have dinner with me, Emma, but taking it as a proposal of marriage was going a bit far, don't you think?' he grated sarcastically.

'You've every right to be annoyed,' she said quietly. 'I'm sorry.'

'I shall have to put him straight—'

'Don't!' She stared at him, her eyes wide, pleading.

'Please.' She caught hold of his hand as he put it back down on the table, covering it with hers in an automatic gesture. 'Please do this for me, Frazer. Jon is only going to be here for two days. I've told him the engagement is secret, so he won't tell anyone else.'

'If he chooses your place as a location for his next film he'll be here for more than two days.'

'I didn't consider that.' She bit down on her lip. 'I wasn't thinking clearly.'

'You can say that again.' His voice was dry. 'Look, I'm not one for playing emotional games. If you want to make the guy feel jealous then choose some other sucker for the task.'

'I don't want to make him jealous!' She took her hand away from his sharply.

'So what are you playing at?'

She swallowed hard. Her eyes were wide and filled with feeling. For a moment she felt like a little girl, hurt, scared. 'I just needed to erect some barriers. I don't expect you to understand, but I had to keep him at a distance.'

She looked towards the bar. Jon was making his way back with their drinks. 'I had no right to involve you. I realise that. I don't know what came over me.' She shrugged helplessly. 'Haven't you ever said or done something on the spur of the moment and then wondered why the hell you did it?'

Frazer didn't get the opportunity to reply to that because Jon returned to the table. 'I took the liberty of getting you a glass of wine, Emma,' he said.

'Thank you.' The alcohol was welcome at this moment. She glanced at Frazer, waiting for him to say something to her ex-husband.

Jon sat down and lifted his glass of whisky in a salute. 'Here's to your future. I hope you will both be very happy,' he said graciously.

Emma squirmed in her chair. Her throat felt unbelievably dry as Frazer met her eyes.

Suddenly an idea born of desperation came to her. 'You know that land you wanted to rent?' she said hurriedly. 'Well, I think I can make a good deal for you on it.'

Frazer stared at her, and in the ensuing moment of silence Emma could hear her heart thumping against her chest, heavy and painful.

'How good?' Frazer asked finally.

'Better than you dared hope for,' she said in an undertone.

'Hey, you two. I was making a toast for your forthcoming wedding!' Jon interrupted. 'Do you think you could forget business for a while?'

There was a moment's hesitation. Then Frazer lifted his glass. 'Sorry, Jon,' he said cheerfully. 'Here's to the future.'

Emma felt her breath escape in a long, pent-up sigh of relief. Her hand wasn't quite steady as she lifted her glass to clink it against Frazer's.

'So, how did you two meet?' Jon asked as he leaned back against his chair and looked from one to the other.

Emma's hand trembled alarmingly and she had to put her glass down.

'How did we meet?' Frazer repeated the question and glanced over at Emma. There was a spark of amusement now in his dark eyes. 'We met over a troublesome goat called Molly. I was returning her from her marauding travels, Emma opened the door, and it was love at first sight.' Frazer reached across and covered her hand with his, just as she had done a few moments earlier. Only where her touch had been pleading his was seductive, and his thumb rubbed over her soft skin in a way that sent shivers racing through her body. 'I thought Emma was the most beautiful woman I had ever seen.'

His voice was low and bewitching. It was as if they were

alone, as if he was speaking directly to her heart. 'I was totally captivated.'

She felt each beat of her heart as it slammed against her chest.

'I knew right there and then that she was the woman I wanted to spend the rest of my life with.'

'But you didn't even know her.' Jon's tone was incredulous. It brought Emma back to reality with a crash.

She pulled her hand away from his. 'No, he didn't. Frazer is a bit of a romantic.'

'That's what you love about me, honey, isn't it?' The humorous glint in Frazer's eyes made her blood pump furiously through her veins. He was enjoying himself, she realised suddenly. Enjoying putting her through hoops and watching her squirm.

'Emma has always been a romantic at heart,' Jon said reflectively.

Emma didn't think it was possible for her to feel any more awkward than she felt at that moment. She was acutely conscious of both men watching her now. Jon with that sad expression in his eyes, and Frazer with that devilish gleam of amusement. 'I suppose that's why she's come running up to Scotland. It appeals to her sense of romance. But honestly, Frazer, Emma is a city girl; I can't see her being happy living a rural life.'

Emma glared at her ex-husband. How dared he discuss her in that patronising, condescending way? 'But then you don't really know me any more, do you, Jon?' she contradicted him crisply.

'Believe it or not, I can decide for myself what I want out of life.' Her voice was laced with sarcasm.

'Oh, you don't need to worry about Emma,' Frazer said dryly.

'She's taken to farming like a dream. Up every morning

with the cockerel and out milking by five a.m. She's a natural.'

'Really?' Jon looked astonished, which wasn't surprising because getting up in the morning had never been Emma's strong point. She certainly didn't get up at five to do any milking. She glared at Frazer. 'Now don't exaggerate, darling,' she said with equal sarcasm. 'I'm never out of bed before five-thirty.'

He grinned at her. 'Well, not if I can help it,' he drawled with seductive emphasis.

She felt her cheeks flood with embarrassed colour. 'You know, I'm going to have to get going,' she murmured, glancing at her watch.

'Do you have to rush off?' Jon asked dolefully.

'Oh, it's a good, healthy life in the country. Early to bed, early to rise,' Frazer answered for her.

Emma's eyes were shimmering with fury as she looked over at him. She was grateful to him for helping her out of a hole, but she wished he would stop with the wisecracks.

She transferred her attention to her ex-husband. 'Yes, I have to go. I'm sorry, Jon. What time are you expecting your location manager to arrive tomorrow?'

Jon shrugged. 'Mid-morning, I think. I'll give you a ring once she arrives, tell you what time you can expect us.'

'Fine. I thought your manager was a man, for some reason.'

She was desperately struggling to keep the conversation on this light level.

'No, Lesley May is all woman.' Jon grinned for a moment. 'And she is very good at her job.'

'Sounds interesting,' Frazer remarked.

'Tell you what,' Jon suggested suddenly, 'why don't the four of us go out for dinner tomorrow night? Somewhere first class...my treat.'

The very idea disturbed Emma intensely. The thought of a whole night like this was just pure torture. 'No, I'm sorry we can't,' she said swiftly. 'Tomorrow is Frazer's evening for...' She looked over at him, wondering what excuse to give. Her eyes moved over the breadth of his shoulders. The suit did fantastic things for an already wonderful body. 'Frazer's night for body-building.'

It was the first thing that came into her head. She felt a certain satisfaction as she noticed his eyes narrow. Well, he had embarrassed her; it was only fitting she should have some retribution, she thought with a smile.

'That's OK, darling,' Frazer cut across her with a smile of his own. 'I don't mind missing my body-building session this once.'

Her smile faded. She should have known better than to try retaliation with a man like Frazer McClarran, she thought helplessly. 'Now, Frazer,' she tried to admonish with firm emphasis, 'you know you just hate to miss those sessions in the gym.'

'No...it's all right.' His voice was airily light. But she could tell from the gleam in his eyes that he was well aware that she was furious with him for accepting the damn invitation. 'My muscles can stand a night off. Besides, we can work out together, later,' he murmured, his voice huskily seductive.

Her skin felt as if it was on fire. She was simply livid. She gave him a very strained smile. 'If you're sure,' she demurred quietly. But she had no intention of going along with this absurd suggestion. She would tell Jon very firmly tomorrow that dinner was out of the question.

'Well, I had better go.' She smiled at her ex-husband. 'See you tomorrow.'

'Haven't you forgotten something?' Frazer stalled her before she could stand up.

She glanced over at him warily.

'My goodnight kiss,' Frazer murmured in a low tone.

Emma stared at him in disbelief. Her body felt as if it was rooted to the chair. Her heart was racing out of control, and her lips felt as if they were tingling as his eyes rested on their softness.

This was ridiculous! He wouldn't dare.

The thought had no sooner entered her mind than he was leaning closer to her. She could see the humour in his dark eyes. She sat stiffly, unsure of what to do.

His lips touched hers. They were soft, gentle, persuasive. The feeling was intensely disturbing. She found herself kissing him back.

It could only have lasted for a second. But it felt incredible.

He pulled away from her and she could only stare at him wordlessly. He didn't look amused now, she noted; he looked very serious. She blinked, then reality returned with a rush as he grinned at her. Now she knew she had really lost her senses. The man was simply trying to wind her up; there was nothing serious about that kiss at all.

'Well, goodnight.' Her voice held a tremor that made her cringe.

'Oh, Em,' Jon stalled her. 'You haven't given me the directions to your place.'

'Sorry, I forgot.' She wished her voice would steady. 'I wrote them down for you.' She opened up her bag and rooted through the contents, finding the piece of paper with the photographs she had brought. She handed them across to him and was dismayed to find her hand was shaking.

She glanced across at Frazer, hoping he might not have noticed. He grinned at her, a teasing, good-natured light in the darkness of his eyes. Of course he had noticed, she realised with a sinking feeling. She gave him a stiff smile. 'Well, goodnight.'

He stood up with her. 'I'll walk you to your car,' he said. 'See you later, Jon. Perhaps you'd like to join the party in the back room?'

Emma didn't wait around to hear Jon's reply. She was

heading out of the bar with as much speed as was decently possible.

Frazer caught up with her as she went down the steps outside.

It had stopped raining, but the pavements and the road gleamed silver in the overhead streetlights, slick with water.

'Hold on a moment,' Frazer said, catching hold of her arm.

'What did you think you were playing at in there?' She swung to face him, her eyes overly bright in the pallor of her face.

'I was playing at being your fiancé. Wasn't that what you pleaded with me to do?' he asked calmly.

'You over-acted the part,' she accused furiously. 'You deliberately set out to embarrass me.'

'I thought I did very well, considering the circumstances,' Frazer replied stoically. 'You were the one who went overboard with the body-building.'

'Oh? And what about all those references to us sharing a bed, and that rubbish about my getting up at five to do the milking?'

'Well, he needed putting in his place. I'm sure you could get up at five a.m. if you wanted to.' Frazer grinned, unabashed. 'And as for the references about us sharing a bed, I was just getting into character. If I was your fiancé, I *would* be sharing your bed.' Frazer's voice dropped to a low, intimate note. 'And I wouldn't be happy about you getting out of it too early, either.' He smiled as he noted the two high spots of colour that burnt on her cheeks now.

'A little bit of subtlety wouldn't have gone amiss.' She tried not to be sidetracked.

'I don't think you have much leeway to preach about subtlety. You were the woman that dropped me into the damn situation in the first place,' Frazer said with incredulity.

'Yes, but you didn't have to accept that dinner invitation, did you? You knew I was trying to get out of it.'

He shrugged. 'After promising me such a good deal on that land of yours, I thought you should get your money's worth. It was the least I could do.' He laughed at her look of outrage. 'You do intend to honour our agreement, I take it?'

'Is that why you've followed me out here? To make sure you get your pound of flesh?'

'Hey!' He caught hold of her arm again as she made to swing away from him. The amusement had died from his eyes and he looked angry now. 'I helped you out in there. You should be thanking me.'

She bit down on her lip. He was right. 'Yes, I know. And I am really grateful,' she said softly, the fire inside her dying. 'You helped me, and I will repay you. I meant what I said about the land.'

He stared at her. Her hair was a wild tumble of colour around very pale skin; her eyes were a brilliant jewel blue. 'That's OK, then,' he said softly.

It started to rain suddenly.

'Oh, no! I've forgotten my umbrella,' she wailed.

Frazer took off the jacket of his suit and held it over her head. 'Where have you parked your car?'

'Just down here.' She nodded in the direction of a dark side-street.

'Come on, then.' He put an arm around her waist and together they ran down the road. She could have told him that her umbrella was only inside the pub doorway, but she didn't. She was quite impressed by the display of chivalry. And acutely conscious of the touch of his hand around her waist, the hard, lean length of his body pressed against hers. As they reached her car she got her keys out of her hand-bag. 'Thank you.' She sounded prim and polite.

'It was the least I could do for my part-time fiancée.'

She smiled. His face seemed very close to hers under the

canopy of the jacket. She found herself remembering the way he had kissed her earlier. She wondered what it would be like to make love with him. The notion made her blood pressure increase dramatically. She stepped back from him abruptly, out into the rain. 'I'll drop you back at the front door of the hotel if you want.'

'OK.' He went around to the passenger door.

She got in and leaned across to open it for him.

They were silent on the short drive around to the front of the building. 'Thank you, once again, for bailing me out tonight,' she said softly as she pulled the car to a standstill.

'That's all right.' He looked across at her. Her face was lit by the bright lights from the hotel. 'Your ex-husband must have hurt you a lot,' he remarked suddenly.

'What makes you say that?'

'Why else would you want to put up such huge barriers.'

The statement was so matter-of-fact that she couldn't argue with it, even if her pride wanted her to. So she didn't reply.

'All I can say is that the man must be a fool.'

She stared at him, her heart thumping. He spoke with such sincerity and warmth. But then Frazer McClarran didn't know the truth behind her marriage break-up. If he did, maybe he would sympathise with her ex-husband, she reminded herself sharply. So she shrugged slender shoulders. 'It wasn't all his fault,' she told him briskly. 'Some people just shouldn't get married, and I'm one of them.'

'You might have told me that before we got engaged,' he said humorously.

'Sorry.' She smiled. 'We'll call the whole thing off once I get my ex-husband off the doorstep tomorrow.'

'What happens if he decides to stay around a bit longer?' Frazer asked quietly. 'For instance if he chooses your residence for his film location.'

'I'll tell him we've quarrelled and the whole thing's off,'

she said without hesitation. 'Don't worry, I wouldn't dream of getting you in any deeper.'

'Just as long as I don't have to walk down the aisle,' he said wryly. 'I don't think I'm the marrying kind myself.'

She laughed. 'Well, then, you're safe with me.'

He reached for the door handle of the car.

'Don't forget your jacket,' she said, holding it out to him.

'Keep it. You'll need it when you get home if this rain keeps up. I'll collect it from you tomorrow.'

She watched as he ran up the steps and into the hotel. The thought of seeing him again tomorrow wasn't altogether unwelcome.

# CHAPTER FOUR

THE sky was a clear forget-me-not-blue. The breeze that rippled over the surface of the loch was warm and spoke of mellow summer days. Emma noticed that the heather was starting to come into bloom, and bright purple and pink swathes lit the mountains. On a sudden impulse she took off her boots and socks and rolled up her trousers to paddle her toes in the clear water.

The water was very cold and the pebbles sharp under her feet, but she didn't care. On a day like today she was glad to be alive. She couldn't remember when she had last felt so happy. There was a zing in the air, a feeling of excitement. Maybe it was just the glorious scenery that filled her spirit with well-being; maybe it was the fact that her ex-husband had visited her this morning and had told her that her property was perfect for his filming requirements. The amount of money he would pay would enable her to refurbish the house, pay the farm labourers and some debts. Life was suddenly filled with new and exciting possibilities. Things were suddenly going her way.

And today Frazer was coming for dinner. He had rung her a little while ago to arrange to collect his jacket, and on impulse she had invited him to stay and eat with her. Back at the house she had a Greek salad in the fridge and a roast of lamb in the oven. It would be a celebration meal, she thought happily. The only black cloud was that she hadn't been able to get out of Jon's dinner invitation—although she had managed to put him off until he came back up from London next week.

Still, it was a small price to pay, Emma thought happily as she turned her face up towards the sun. She supposed that once her ex-husband returned to Scotland she would have to tell him that her engagement was off. She couldn't expect Frazer to keep up the pretence. She turned her mind away from the disconcerting knowledge that Jon was going to be around a lot now. She didn't want to dwell on the complexities of that situation. It was enough that for the time being her financial problems were sorted out.

Although it was just mid-September, it was really very warm today. Warm enough to swim.

The notion was tempting. She looked around her. She was completely alone, with just the vastness of the countryside and a few sheep munching on the bracken for company. Frazer wasn't due at the house for another hour or so. Enough time for her to be showered and changed with everything ready.

She went to the banks of the loch and quickly stepped out of her combat trousers and peeled off her fleece, draping them safely over a rock before going back into the water in just her bra and pants.

The water was very cold and clear. She could see her toes sinking between the sharp sand and pebbles on the bed of the loch. She hesitated when she got up to her waist. The water felt freezing against her warm skin. Taking a deep breath, she took the plunge and submerged herself. After the initial shock it was very pleasant—exhilarating, in fact.

She swam for a few moments, her breathing loud in the silence of the day. Then she turned on her back and floated lazily, looking up at the beauty of a clear blue sky.

People in Scotland were lovely, she thought. Everyone had been so friendly and welcoming, especially this morning when she had gone into the village to get some shopping for her dinner with Frazer.

Mrs Murray had beamed at her as if she were a long-lost daughter. 'Having a romantic dinner?' she had asked with a wink of her eye as Emma had put a bottle of red wine on the counter and some candles.

'No, just entertaining a friend,' Emma had said hastily.

'Run up an account, if you like,' Mrs Murray had offered with a broad smile. 'We've got some very good-quality champagne in stock—oh, and some Belgian chocolates. I happen to know they go down very well…if you know what I mean?' Then she had winked again.

Emma hadn't taken her up on the offer. She preferred to pay for whatever she got there and then. Champagne had seemed a bit excessive for a friendly dinner, but she had bought the chocolates. More because it had seemed to please Mrs Murray than anything else.

She frowned for a moment as she thought about their conversation. Now that she analysed it, maybe it had been a trifle odd. Why had Mrs Murray kept winking at her like that? Perhaps the woman had an affliction of her eye, a nervous twitch?

'Emma.' The stern voice calling across the loch brought her back to the present with a jump. She turned over to tread water, her eyes moving towards the bank.

Frazer stood there, his hands on his hips. He was wearing a blue shirt tucked into his blue jeans. A breeze played through his hair, ruffling the dark curly texture.

She swam a little closer. 'Hello. You're early!' She smiled at him shyly, keeping her body submerged beneath the water. What she wore was no more revealing than a bikini, but even so she felt a little flustered at being caught out like this.

'Have you been into the village this morning?' he demanded abruptly.

'Yes, I went to do some shopping.' She frowned, wondering why he seemed so angry.

'And you just couldn't keep quiet,' he accused grimly.

'I'm sorry?' She blinked some water out of her eyes. She hadn't got the faintest clue what he was talking about.

'It's a bit late to be sorry!' He raked an impatient hand through his hair. 'I agreed to go along with your ridiculous charade on the understanding it was just between us. I didn't expect to go into Glenmarrin today and have the whole damn community congratulate me on my engagement!'

'What?' Emma's voice rose in horror. Forgetting modesty, she stood up out of the water. 'I didn't tell them! How could you think for one moment I would do that?'

'Maybe it has something to do with the fact that your husband is going to be sticking around here for a while longer?' he grated. 'I hear you've got what you wanted and he's going to use this place as the location for his film.'

'Ex-husband.' Emma corrected. 'And, well…yes, he is…' Emma struggled to think straight. 'Who told you that?'

'Your ex-husband told me when I bumped into him this morning at the supermarket. At the same time as Mrs Murray was congratulating me on our engagement.'

'Oh, hell!'

'Exactly.' Frazer glared at her.

'Did you put her straight?' Emma's teeth chattered, but she didn't know if it was from cold or mortification.

'No, your ex was listening to every word. Though heaven knows why I didn't just go ahead and tell them the whole thing was a joke, or something.'

For a moment his eyes slipped over her figure. Her skin was a honey-brown, and it glistened with silvery water in the light of the sun. 'I mean, it's not as if I owe you something, is it? I agreed to help you out of a tight spot, but I didn't agree to tell the whole community that we are about to be hitched.' He was trying not to notice the way her lacy bra revealed full high breasts over a narrow ribcage and a tiny waist. Or the way her hips curved in a womanly shape that was accentuated by very pretty lacy pants.

She pushed her hand through her hair, wringing out the

excess water from the long curly length as she walked up onto the shore. 'I know you didn't,' she said quietly. 'And I'm sorry. But I assure you that whatever they have heard in the village, they haven't heard it from me.'

'Well, somebody has said something. Your ex-husband assured me it wasn't him.'

'You asked him?'

'Yes, as we left the supermarket. About the same time as Mrs McCall from the post office shouted across to me that she was dusting off her hat for my big day.'

Emma cringed. 'I don't know what to say...except thank you. It was very gentlemanly of you not to tell everyone it was all a...misunderstanding.'

'Damn stupid, you mean.' He frowned, unable to concentrate on their conversation. She was a total distraction, standing in front of him like that.

He reached behind him and picked up her clothes. 'Here, cover yourself up,' he said impatiently. 'You look as if you're about to freeze to death.'

'Thanks.' She took her clothes from him and pulled the warm woollen fleece over her head before stepping into her trousers.

Her legs were incredibly long and shapely, he noticed.

'Jon must have said something by mistake,' she said as she pulled the drawstring waist on her trousers and tied it. 'It probably wasn't intentional on his part. I did ask him not to say anything and I don't think he would have deliberately gone against my wishes. He's quite trustworthy.'

'You've got a high regard for him, haven't you? Considering he broke your heart,' Frazer grated dryly.

'Who says he broke my heart?' She was instantly on the defensive.

'You did last night, when you collared me for the role of fiancé.'

'I didn't say any such thing! That was your assessment, not mine. I told you our divorce was by mutual agreement.'

Frazer grunted with disbelief. 'So what exactly is going on between you and Jon Sinclair? What have I unwittingly got myself in the middle of?'

'Nothing's going on. I told you, the farm needs a lot of money spending on it, and my contact with my ex-husband is purely business—'

'If it was purely business, you wouldn't have needed a bogus fiancé,' Frazer cut across her quickly. 'I do think you owe me a better explanation than that.'

She nodded, the fire inside her dying. He had every right to be annoyed. 'If you must know I did it because...because Jon wants me back, and it was the only way I could think of to keep him at bay.'

Frazer was quiet for a moment. 'I thought you said that your ex-husband had remarried?'

'He had. Apparently his marriage has broken up.'

'You must be very tempted to go back to him,' he remarked coolly.

'Nothing could be further from the truth!'

'Oh, come on, Emma. If you can't be honest with me, at least be honest with yourself.' His voice was scathing. 'You dreamt up a fiancé from out of nowhere to help *you* keep your distance from *him*, not the other way round.'

Her heart seemed to miss a beat at that remark, and bounce crazily against her chest. That wasn't true, was it? She stared at him. Her eyes were a vivid, vulnerable shade of blue in a face that was suddenly very pale. Suddenly she wasn't sure. Had this man, who didn't know her at all, fathomed exactly what was in her heart? Something she wasn't able to do herself. 'No.' She shook her head. 'I'd never be crazy enough to want Jon back.'

'Because he hurt you so much?' Frazer surmised gently.

She met his eyes directly again, but this time she was angry. 'Yes, all right, because he hurt me,' she admitted tightly. 'Satisfied?'

Frazer shrugged. 'It's none of my business.'

'No. It's not. So will you please stop with the psychoanalysing?'

'I'm not interested enough to psychoanalyse you,' Frazer retorted firmly.

She frowned. That remark had hurt. Why should it hurt? she wondered. This man meant nothing to her.

Frazer watched the play of emotions over her face, and frowned. He suddenly wished he could take those words back. Emma was having the strangest effect on him. He didn't know her, yet one moment she irritated him wildly, the next he felt the sudden need to protect her—like last night in the pub, and this morning in the supermarket. The way she was looking at him now stirred feelings within him similar to the way he felt when one of his animals was wounded and looked at him with huge doe eyes.

'Well, maybe that's not entirely true,' he conceded softly.

There was a moment's confusion in her eyes. Then she said tersely, 'You're just being polite now because you think you've hurt my feelings.'

'And have I?'

'No, you damn well haven't.' Her eyes sparkled mutinously.

He grinned. 'Good. I'm glad we've got that sorted out.'

When he smiled like that it lit the darkness of his eyes like warm Guinness. She had never met anyone who had such dark eyes.

She felt her anger evaporate. 'I don't know why we're arguing over this anyway,' she said with a sigh. 'My reasons for what I did are quite irrelevant.' She turned to put on her boots and socks. 'I've got you into this stupid predicament and I'll have to get you out of it. Preferably before the whole of the town have gone out and bought themselves new hats.'

'I think speed is important,' Frazer agreed.

She slanted a wry look up at him. 'So I suppose holding

fire for a week is out of the question? I couldn't get out of that dinner invitation with Jon and his location manager.'

'You must be joking!'

She grinned mischievously. 'Yes, all right. Although you were keen to offer last night, if I remember rightly. You even offered to give up your body-building session, and you know how important it is to you,' she finished with a giggle.

Frazer laughed and shook his head. 'And I was only drinking Coke! But last night was different, Emma. It was a game between us, not the whole community.'

'Yes, of course it was; you don't need to tell me that.' She went back to tying the laces on her boots. 'I did say that if Jon chose my residence for his film location then we could just tell him we've had an argument and have split up. As you know, I never expected you to carry on the pretence for more than a few days anyway. I mean, I'm really grateful that you've done it at all.' She straightened up and looked at him, an earnest light in her eyes. 'And I'm thankful that you didn't drop me in it when you were in the supermarket with Jon today. You would have had every right to tell him and Mrs Murray that I'd made the whole thing up.'

'Yes,' he agreed quietly. 'And I meant it when I said I don't know why in the hell I didn't.' His eyes flicked over her. All the womanly curves were covered up now, in loose, baggy clothing. But for some reason she still looked seductive. Her hair was starting to dry in red-gold waves around her face, wild and luxurious.

'Yes...well.' Emma shrugged awkwardly, feeling suddenly embarrassed when she thought about the dreadful position she had placed him in. 'Thank you for not doing that.'

Frazer didn't reply.

She shivered. The day was clouding over and the brief

spell of warmth had disappeared. She was suddenly conscious of the fact that her hair and her clothes were damp.

'You better get back to the house before you catch pneumonia,' he said softly.

'And before the dinner burns.' She looked up at him. 'You do still want to join me for dinner?'

'Yes, of course. Why wouldn't I?'

She shrugged. 'I wouldn't blame you if you wanted to keep your distance.'

He smiled. 'I might not want to go through with the engagement, but we can still be just good friends, can't we?'

She smiled back. 'I don't see why not. I mean, we are neighbours.'

She lifted her keys from the rock where she had left them and together they walked back up the hill in the direction of the house.

The wind was getting up, and grey clouds swirled ominously over the distant dark shape of Daniels Hall. Her inheritance, she thought with a sharp burst of pride.

'Do you really think that my uncle left this place to me with the intention of trying to heal his past mistakes?' she asked Frazer impulsively.

He looked over at her quizzically.

'You remember you said something to that effect when we had coffee together the other day,' she reminded him.

'Yes, I remember.' He nodded. 'I don't know, Emma, but it's a possibility. Ethan wasn't a bad man. Damned irritating, but underneath the gruff exterior I think he meant well.'

She stumbled on an uneven piece of bracken and Frazer reached out, catching her hand in his to steady her.

'Heavens, you're cold!' he said, squeezing the small hand in the warmth of his.

'Yes.' She hadn't realised how cold she was until he touched her. She was glad when he didn't let go of her.

'It's too late in the season to be swimming in that loch,' Frazer said crisply. 'And before I forget, you shouldn't swim too far out of your depth, especially when you're on your own. I know it's not the sea, but, even so, there can be strong eddying currents.'

Emma stopped and stared at him in horror. 'That wasn't where my father drowned, was it?'

'No. Your father died at sea, on a fishing expedition from Glenmarrin. The boat overturned in a sudden storm.'

'I thought that was how it had happened, but I never really knew.' She stared at him. 'It's good having someone to talk to about it,' she admitted hesitantly. 'I used to ask my mother about him, but she just wanted to forget about the past, and I suppose I don't blame her for that. He did treat her badly.'

'Dreadfully,' Frazer agreed. He gave her hand a gentle tug. 'Come on, I think it's going to rain.'

They walked on for a while in silence.

'What does your mother think about you inheriting your father's estate?' Frazer asked suddenly.

'My mother died two years ago, when I was going through my divorce.'

'I'm sorry.' He squeezed her hand.

She looked up at him. The gentle understanding in his voice made her heart quicken.

The sky was darkening by the minute. A few drops of rain splattered onto her face.

'Come on.' Frazer pulled at her hand and they set off running. The wind that cut against their faces was scented with the dampness of the heather and the salt of the distant sea.

They practically fell in through her front door. Emma certainly wasn't cold now. Her blood was zinging through her veins like a central heating system. Frazer looked at her and smiled. Her cheeks were glowing with warmth and her hair had dried in a mass of luxuriant waves. She smiled back at him, a cautious slow smile that reminded him of the sun coming out from behind the clouds.

He watched as she moistened her lips. They looked soft and very inviting. He wanted to kiss her. In fact he would have liked to take her into his arms and explore the wondrous delights of the curvaceous body he knew was hiding under that baggy clothing.

Instead he stepped back, but it took every ounce of his self-control. 'Something smells good in here.'

'Yes, roast lamb.' Emma turned away from him. She felt disconcerted. She had thought that he was going to kiss her, and had welcomed the idea. The disappointment she felt at being wrong was out of all proportion.

'Why don't you go and change out of those damp clothes and I'll go and check on the oven?' he suggested.

'OK, thanks.' It was a relief to head upstairs, away from him.

She didn't get changed immediately, but sat on the side of her bed, trying to make some sense of the feelings that had assailed her a moment ago. She didn't want to get involved with Frazer McClarran, she reminded herself. She didn't want any serious involvement with any man. She couldn't put herself through that again. Once with Jon had been enough. Not that one kiss meant you had to get serious. A kiss wouldn't have undermined her good intentions.

She sighed and looked at her reflection in the dressing table mirror. 'Let's face it, Emma,' she told herself in a soft undertone. 'He probably just doesn't fancy you. Especially after the scare he got when he went into the village this morning.' Her lips curved in a moment of pure amusement as she pictured the scene. She thought she knew Frazer well enough to know he would have been horrified by everyone's assumptions. Mrs Murray had told her categorically that he was a zealous bachelor. Her equilibrium restored, she got up and opened her wardrobe doors to select a clean pair of jeans and a white cotton top.

When she returned to the kitchen Frazer had the joint out of the oven and was prodding it with a long fork.

'How's it doing?' she asked brightly.

'It's done.' He turned and looked at her. How did she manage to look so damn sexy in a pair of jeans and a close-fitting top? he wondered, with a certain amount of irritation. He wasn't going to get involved with her, he told himself swiftly. For one thing she was the type who had 'serious' written all over her; for another she probably wasn't going to stay in these parts very long. As soon as the winter closed in she'd be back down to London with a whimper of relief. And the third most important reason why he wouldn't get involved with her was that he reckoned she was still in love with her ex-husband, and he wasn't going to play at love on the rebound. Friendship, he told himself firmly, was all he could have with Emma Sinclair.

'Perhaps you wouldn't mind carving the meat while I set the table?' she asked.

'Certainly.'

Emma opened the door through from the kitchen to the dining room. This part of the house was not in bad repair. The kitchen was a pleasant, old-fashioned farm kitchen, with a large range and a red-tiled floor. The dining room was small and cosy. She had lit the fire in there earlier, but it was dying out now. She threw on another few pieces of wood and stoked the flames, before turning her attention to the table.

When Frazer appeared in the doorway a few moments later, the large table was set. Emma had put wrought-iron candlesticks in the centre and the red candle light flickered invitingly.

'Is your electricity on the blink again?' Frazer asked wryly.

'No, I fixed the electricity when you left the other night.' Emma put her hands on her hips. 'It was just a fuse in the box down in the cellar.'

'There's no end to your talents,' he said quietly.

'I'm self-sufficient, if that's what you mean,' she said brightly.

Frazer looked as if he was about to flick on the overhead light.

'I thought we'd eat by candlelight. It's more relaxing,' Emma said firmly. 'That way I'm not reminded quite so starkly that this room needs decorating.'

He grinned at that.

She pulled out a chair. 'Make yourself comfortable.'

'Thanks.' He watched as she went back through to the kitchen. A moment later some soft music filtered through from the CD player.

'I just love classical music, don't you?' she asked as she came back through and put their salads on the table.

'Most of it,' Frazer agreed cautiously. 'Though sometimes I've got to be in the mood for it.'

'I know what you mean.' She sat down opposite him. 'If you're feeling sad, it can make you even more melancholy. I once cried my way through *Swan Lake*.'

Frazer watched the way the candlelight reflected in her eyes, played over the soft perfection of her creamy skin. What had been going on in her life at that point? he wondered. Her divorce?

'But then if you're feeling happy it lifts you up even further.'

'What other music do you like?' he asked.

'I like contemporary Celtic music. I find the tones go well with my surroundings here, kind of moody and haunting.'

Frazer's expression was serious for a moment. 'Don't romanticise this place, Emma,' he said cautiously. 'It may look beautiful when the sun is shining, but in the depths of winter, believe me, it's bleak.'

'I'm realistic enough to know that much, Frazer,' she told him quickly.

There was a feeling of tension between them for a moment, an emotion Emma couldn't explain. Frazer's eyes held hers for a long moment, then dropped, and she wondered if she had imagined the atmosphere.

'As long as you know what you're letting yourself in for.' He reached over and poured them both a glass of red wine. 'Most years we get a lot of snow, and it comes early. You'll probably have to dig yourself out some mornings.'

'I'll survive,' she said with a smile. 'How far away is your house?'

'Six miles as the crow flies, but it's an eight-mile drive on these small, twisty mountain roads. Too far to come and dig you out.'

'That's a pity,' she murmured huskily.

She looked down at her food, surprised at herself. Was she flirting with him? It certainly sounded like it.

'And have you always lived here?' She made a frantic attempt to sound nonchalant.

He shook his head. 'I went to university in Edinburgh, trained as a vet. When I qualified, I went to Australia for a couple of years.'

'I thought you would have studied agriculture,' Emma said in surprise.

'So did my father.' Frazer smiled. 'But animals have always been my first love.'

'But you've ended up in farming?'

'My father died and the family farm came to me.' Frazer shrugged. 'I guess it was my destiny. I always knew I'd inherit the estate. I'm the only son, and my sister Helen certainly didn't want it. She's happily married to a solicitor and lives in France.'

'So you didn't mind coming back from Australia and taking over?'

'Hell, no. I love the work. Farming in general isn't paying a great deal...as I'm sure you will find out for yourself, if you stay here for any length of time. But I've diversified

I've invested heavily into starting a stud farm. It's been fairly successful and I enjoy working with the horses.' He looked over at her. 'You'll have to come over and take a look around.'

'I'd love to.' She took a sip of her wine. 'I suppose we should sort out the little matter of our phoney engagement first.'

'I suppose we should.'

'What do you want me to do?' She looked over at him. 'I could go into Mrs Murray's shop, as that seems to be the hub of the gossip, and just tell her the truth.' Emma wrinkled her nose at the thought. 'I'd feel very stupid, but then I suppose I deserve to feel like that.'

'I don't think you deserve to feel like that,' Frazer said kindly.

'Thanks.' She smiled at him. He was really very nice, and extremely handsome. She looked hurriedly away from those dark eyes.

'When is your ex-husband coming back?'

'A week on Monday, with a whole entourage of people. They'll be starting to get the house ready for filming.'

'And where will they be staying?'

'The Traveller's Rest, I suppose.'

'So Jon isn't expecting to stay here, with you?'

'Good heavens, no!' She was horrified by the suggestion. She stood up and started to clear away their dishes. 'To be honest, I'm trying not to think about the details too much. I'm just trying to focus on the fact that I need the money.'

She went through to the kitchen to get their main course.

'I wonder what Jon is focusing on?' Frazer followed her from the table and leant against the doorway, watching her.

'Making a good film, I would hope. He's very ambitious, and he has always put his career first.'

'Is that why your marriage fell apart?'

The quietly asked question made her heart thump uneasily against her breast. 'No, it's not.' She looked over at him, and her eyes were wide and shimmering with an expression of pain. 'I'd prefer it if you didn't ask me about that,' she said softly.

He shrugged. 'I'm sorry. I didn't mean to pry.'

'It's not that...' She struggled with a wealth of different emotions. She didn't want to offend him by being aloof, but she couldn't talk about the real reason Jon had left her. It was far too raw a subject. How could you blurt out something as deep and as painful as not being able to bear the man you had loved a child when you knew it was the one thing in the world he had wanted?

'It's OK, Emma,' Frazer cut across her gently. 'I shouldn't have asked. I understand. Really, I do.' He came across and stood beside her. 'Whose meal is that?' he asked, looking down at the plate she had been heaping potatoes on.

'Yours.'

'I like potatoes, Emma, but don't you think you're going a bit overboard?' He grinned at her.

'I meant to put them on a serving plate.' She watched as he sorted the error out and then picked up the plates to carry them through to the other room for her.

'This looks very good,' he said as he took his seat opposite her and started tucking in. 'You're an excellent cook.'

'Thank you.' She glanced down at her plate. She knew he was making a solicitous effort to cover her momentary distress and she was grateful.

A few moments ago she had been starving; now her appetite seemed to have vanished. She picked at her food.

'You know, if you want, we can keep our bogus engagement going for another week or so,' Frazer suggested tentatively as he looked across at her, noting the troubled shadows in her eyes. 'It won't help much, but it might ease things for you enough to get you through this dinner engagement with your ex-husband.'

'You'd accompany me to dinner as my fiancé?' She looked over at him hopefully.

He nodded. 'If it would help?'

'It would.' She let out her breath in a sigh. 'It's funny, but last night in the pub I couldn't think of anything worse than dinner with Jon and you. But today I'm really grateful for the offer.'

'Well, I suppose today you're in even deeper, aren't you?' Frazer said with a shake of his head. 'Jon has told you he has selected your premises for his film. You're going to have to get used to having him around again.'

'Yes.' She looked at him seriously. 'You really don't mind keeping up our pretence for a week? It's more than I dared hope for.'

'No, I don't mind. Just as long as we break things off immediately after the dinner, before Ede gets back.'

'Who's Ede? Your girlfriend?' Emma looked at him in consternation.

'My aunt. She's on holiday in Greece at the moment, I'm glad to say, because if she was here and heard the news of my engagement the church would be booked by now and the invitations sent out.'

'Really?' Emma grinned. She was relieved to hear that he hadn't been talking about a girlfriend. So relieved that it seemed to have restored her good spirits.

'Yes, really. Ede has recently taken it into her head that it is time I got married. She has set me up on blind dates, introduced me to friends' daughters, and altogether made me squirm with embarrassment she has been so blatant in her matchmaking.'

Emma grimaced. 'There's nothing worse.'

'Exactly,' Frazer agreed with feeling. 'She has been trying for weeks to interest me in some girl called Nicole. She wants me to accompany her to Ruth and Mark's wedding. I have determinedly refused to even meet her. Thank God

I'm Mark's best man, because as such I don't really require a date.'

'You could just arrange your own date,' Emma suggested. She was certain that there would be no shortage of willing offers. Not with his looks and personality.

'If I do that, things will become even more complicated. Ede will get it into her head that I'm going to marry the girl. The last woman I dated was convinced I was going to pop the question because Ede invited her round for some supper and told her I was crazy about her but was too shy to say anything.'

'And were you?'

Frazer met her eyes wryly. 'Do I strike you as the shy type?'

Emma laughed. 'Ede sounds as if she means business.'

'Believe me. She does.' Frazer reached for his glass of wine. 'I can't tell you how thankful I am that she's in Greece. If Ede was in Glenmarrin we'd have serious problems.'

Emma lifted her glass. 'Here's to Ede. She sounds a delightful character. May she enjoy the Greek sunshine for a while longer.'

# CHAPTER FIVE

FRAZER reined in his horse and watched Emma from his vantage point at the top of the ridge. Her hair was very red in the afternoon sunlight. She certainly stood out from the men who worked alongside her, and it wasn't just her hair. She worked twice as hard as the men, running with lithe, fluid movements to herd an errant sheep into a pen. The stubborn animal ran past the gate, but, undeterred, Emma changed direction to send him back where she wanted him. Frazer couldn't help noticing that the jeans she wore were moulded in against a very feminine figure, and the blue T-shirt was tight against a shapely outline.

He urged his horse on, irritated with himself for noticing. He rode in to help her, heading the sheep back where she wanted him so she could slam the gate shut.

'Thanks.' She shaded her eyes to look up at him. She was out of breath, he noticed, her breasts heaving slightly under the T-shirt.

'You're welcome.' His voice was curt. He looked over at the two farm labourers with her. Neither of them were out of breath, he noticed wryly. Mind, one of them was Brian Robinson, and he put himself out for nobody.

'You could do with a dog,' he said.

She grinned. 'Possibly. But would I be able to handle a working dog? All those whistles and commands you've got to learn.'

Frazer was starting to think that this woman could handle anything. She seemed to surprise him every time they met. He cleared his throat and slanted a look over at the labourers, who were leaning against the fence listening.

'Congratulations on your engagement, Mr McClarran,' Brian said. 'I suppose we'll be calling you boss soon.'

'I don't think that's very likely, Brian. But thanks for your good wishes.'

For a moment the men continued just to stand there, then, as if Frazer's dark-eyed look disconcerted them, they suddenly straightened and went back to work.

'You don't much care for Brian Robinson, do you, Frazer?'

'I think he's trouble.' Frazer's eyes drifted over to the man. He was stacking some bales of hay up against a fence. Although relatively young, at thirty years of age he was losing his hair. He was also well renowned for losing his temper. 'I'd keep a close eye on him, if I were you.'

'Brian's all right.' Emma walked across to stroke the neck of his horse. It was a magnificent animal, with a black glossy coat and a well-shaped head. Probably a very expensive thoroughbred.

'So what can I do for you, Frazer?'

He reached into the inside pocket of his jacket and brought out an envelope. 'I saw Ruth in town this morning and she asked me to give you this.' He handed it down to her.

'Ruth?'

'My friend Mark's fiancée.'

Emma opened the envelope and turned the gilt-edged card over in her hand in perplexity.

Mr and Mrs Gary Martin
request the pleasure of
your company at the marriage
of their daughter
Ruth
to
Mr Mark Wells.

How had she managed to get invited to a wedding when she didn't know either the bride or the groom?

Frazer dismounted. 'I saw Mark yesterday and he was ribbing me about my whirlwind romance.'

'You didn't tell him the truth?'

'No.' Frazer was quiet for a moment. Then he said briskly. 'Ruth gave me the invitation this morning. She said she was going to post it, but then figured it would save time to give it to me. The wedding is this Saturday.'

'Yes, I can see that.' Emma sighed.

'If you don't want to go…'

'Do you want me to go?' Emma was torn. There was a part of her that would have liked to go to the wedding and meet Frazer's friends. But then, as he had said the other night, he didn't really need a partner. 'I suppose it's taking our make-believe engagement one step further,' she said softly. 'Complicating things further.'

'Yes, I guess you're right,' Frazer said decisively.

'So I'll give my polite regrets, say that I'm unable to attend?'

'That might be for the best.'

Emma felt a weight of disappointment at his reply. What was wrong with her? she wondered angrily. Of course she couldn't attend this wedding. She didn't know anyone and she wasn't really Frazer's fiancée. She was being ridiculous even contemplating it.

'But then again,' Frazer said softly, 'if you'd like to come, it would be fun. It promises to be an exceptional day. There will be nearly two hundred guests. I think everyone from the village is going.'

Emma was silent. She didn't know what to say.

'Actually, Emma,' Frazer said gently, 'I'd really like you to come.'

She looked up at him and smiled. 'In that case, I'll put my acceptance in the post today.'

Her smile was radiant; he felt the warmth of it like the sunshine on his back.

'I have something else for you.' He took out his wallet, opened it and brought out a photograph.

Emma looked down at it. It was an old black and white portrait. 'That's your father.' Frazer pointed to the man on the left. 'Ethan is standing next to him, and that's your grandfather behind them.'

Emma stared at the photograph, studying her father's face intently. He looked sternly at the camera, a proud, almost defiant glint in the darkness of his eyes.

'Where did you get this?' she whispered.

'I was round at my aunt's house last night. I go over occasionally to check on the property while she's away. Photography is something of a hobby for Ede; she seems to have everything that ever happened in the village catalogued in her study. Fêtes, christenings, weddings, funerals—they're all there.' He shrugged. 'It suddenly struck me that if I looked hard enough there would probably be a photo of your father, and sure enough there was.'

'Won't she mind you taking it?'

'No, Ede's not like that. She'll be delighted you've found some pleasure in it.'

Emma looked up at him. Men had brought her chocolates and flowers, expensive gifts sometimes, but nothing meant as much as this photograph. She was overwhelmed by it. 'Thank you, Frazer,' she said softly. 'It means a lot to me.'

'I thought you'd like it.' He sounded offhand.

A soft breeze caught her hair and she pushed it back from her face. He noticed how long her fingers were. She wore no rings.

'Have you heard anything from your ex-husband?'

'He rang last night.' She grimaced. 'Said he might be up here earlier than next Monday. Apparently time is money, and he wants to try and start filming as soon as possible.'

She ran a soothing hand over his horse's neck as he fidgeted impatiently.

'He's a beautiful animal. What do you call him?'

'Eco Warrior.'

Emma wrinkled her nose. 'What kind of a name is that?'

He grinned. 'It's a thoroughbred's name.'

'Can I ride him for a minute?'

Frazer hesitated. 'Yes, but I'd better hold the reins for you. He's very highly strung.'

Emma handed him the photograph. 'Will you keep this safe for a moment?'

He took it from her and put it back in his wallet. She had hoisted herself up in the saddle before he could help her. She gave the horse a gentle nudge and it took off. She heard Frazer's startled exclamation as she whistled past him, down the hill at speed, her hair flying behind her. There was a small stream at the end of the field and she cleared it in one bound.

Frazer felt his heart turn over as she kept on riding towards the tall hedge at the bottom of the paddock. If the horse jumped, she could fall and break her neck.

He had started to run after her when she reined in the animal and turned him with an ease that would have done an expert proud. Frazer halted in his tracks.

'That was wonderful.' She smiled at him as she rode back at a more sedate pace.

'I suppose you think that was funny?' he grated furiously.

'What do you mean?' She batted wide, innocent eyes at him as she dismounted and handed him the reins back. 'You look pale, Frazer. You weren't worried about me, were you?'

'I was more worried about the horse,' he said sarcastically. 'Where did you learn to ride like that anyway?'

Her eyes sparkled mischievously. 'You have a very low

opinion of us city girls, Frazer. Why did you assume I couldn't ride?'

'I shouldn't assume anything where you're concerned, should I?' He grinned. 'Don't tell me. Your brothers are expert horsemen and you wanted to keep up with them?'

'No. Actually, Jon taught me to ride,' Emma admitted. 'We lived for a while on a ranch in California.'

'Sounds very glamorous.'

Emma shrugged. 'I liked California.' She was quiet for a moment. What she didn't tell Frazer was that her year there had been a gruelling round of doctors and specialists. Jon had insisted she saw the best people. Each time her hopes had been raised, only to be dashed again as each of them in turn had told her the same thing: she would never have a child.

She took a deep breath. 'Seeing as you're out here, do you want to tell me what piece of my land you're interested in renting?' She changed the subject abruptly.

'I'll show you.' He led the horse up the hill and she followed him after a moment's hesitation.

'Our boundary fence is there.' He pointed across the rolling countryside. 'I'm interested in the land that runs from there down to the banks of the loch.'

'Why that particular piece of land?'

'It's convenient.'

She sat down on a rock and looked down over the ruggedly beautiful landscape. 'The view is fabulous up here, isn't it?'

Frazer sat down next to her. 'I take it you're not missing London yet?'

'Not at all.' She breathed the clear air in deeply. The breeze was sharp, tinged with pine and heather. The blue sky had a few clouds scudding over it, their dark shadows reflecting on the ruffled waters of the loch and the different shades of the green fields.

They didn't speak for a while. The only sound was the

wind in the trees and the soft munching as his horse pulled idly at a few tufts of grass.

'What did you do in London?'

'I was PA to an executive producer at a television company.'

'And you really think you're going to be happy stuck out here?' He shook his head. 'It can be a bleak, lonely life, Emma.'

'So you've said.' She turned and looked at him. 'But I'll tell you something, Frazer. A person can be lonely when they're surrounded by people. A city life can be a very solitary one. I used to get up at seven and take the tube to work. Nobody spoke. Sometimes if you wished a person good morning they would look at you as if you were about to mug them.'

Frazer smiled.

'You might think I'm joking, but it's true. Everyone was in a hurry. Then I'd get to work, and it was nothing but discussions about deadlines, budgets and rating figures.'

'But you had friends that you saw, surely?'

'Yes. But we were all working such long hours that we usually didn't get together until the weekend.' She frowned. 'I was living my life for the weekends, and life is too short for that.'

'I've got something awful to tell you,' Frazer said quietly.

She turned to look at him.

'Working on a farm, you don't get weekends.'

Her eyes moved over the handsome contours of his face, the gentle light in his dark eyes. 'It doesn't matter,' she said quietly. 'When you're happy inside, happy with what you are doing, it doesn't matter.'

'I hope you feel like that when we get snowed in.'

Emma grinned. 'Are you trying to get rid of me?'

'No.' He reached and touched her face. The sensation sent shivers running through her, delicious shivers of excitement and desire. His face was very close to hers. If she leaned a little closer she would be in his arms. She wanted him to kiss her, wanted it so much that it disturbed her intensely.

'On the contrary, I'm getting used to having you around.'

His voice was husky. Then abruptly he stood up. 'I'd better go. I'll speak to you before Saturday, to arrange what we are doing as regards the wedding.'

'OK.' She really tried not to be disappointed that he was moving away from her. 'I'll have to go and buy myself something to wear; I've only got a couple of days.'

His lips curved in an attractive grin. 'Are you trying to tell me that out of all those clothes that were strewn over your study the other night you don't have anything to wear?'

She nodded and stood up. 'That's exactly right. Anyway, I don't want to let you down. I'm supposed to be your fiancée; I'll have to make a good impression on your friends.'

'I think you'll do that no matter what you wear,' he said quietly.

Emma felt her heart beating loudly against her chest. The way he was looking at her made her feel almost light-headed.

There was silence between them for a moment. Then Frazer said impulsively, 'You know, it might be a good idea if we were to have dinner together again, some time before this wedding. We should really get to know each other a little better if we're to pass as an engaged couple.'

'Maybe you're right,' she agreed happily, glad of any excuse to see him again before Saturday.

'How about tonight?'

'Tonight would be perfect.'

He nodded, then turned away to pick up the reins of his horse and swing himself up in the saddle. 'There's a good restaurant at Castle Howth. It's quite a drive, but worth it for the food. Can I pick you up at seven-thirty?'

'I'll look forward to it,' she said honestly.

He took the photograph that he had brought for her out of his pocket and handed it back to her.

'See you later, then.'

Emma watched as he rode away from her, then she looked down at the photograph. Three men whom she had never met, yet they seemed familiar to her. She smiled. Fate was very strange.

Without them she wouldn't be here now. Wouldn't have met Frazer.

She stood alone on the mountainside, but for the first time ever she felt as if she belonged somewhere.

# CHAPTER SIX

THE restaurant was set in the elegant surroundings of a small castle perched high on the craggy cliffs above the ocean.

Frazer had secured the best table in the house. A secluded alcove from which they could look out towards the sea. It was a clear, moonlit night and the water sparkled and danced as if a thousand silver coins glittered over its surface.

'It's rumoured that Mary Queen of Scots spent several nights here with her lover. They still have her room in the west tower, laid out just as it was then, with the original four-poster bed. You can take a look at it before we leave, if you want.'

Emma turned her attention away from the window. Her eyes held Frazer's across the flickering candlelight. 'Was that a proposition?' she asked with a smile.

He grinned. 'No, it wasn't. But maybe it should have been. I must be slipping.' For a moment the humour left the darkness of his eyes. 'You do look very beautiful tonight, Emma. Very desirable.'

'Thank you.' She felt heat rising inside her body. Her eyes moved away from his. She wished she hadn't made that joke now. She felt suddenly uncertain, scared. It was crazy to feel such a fierce surge of trepidation when she was in the company of a man she had decided she liked enormously, but she couldn't help it.

They had enjoyed a wonderful evening. The conversation had been light and amusing, Frazer had made her laugh, and she had felt very much on the same wavelength as him. But in amongst those light moments there had been a deeper current between them. It was there now. Every time she glanced over at him she felt the heat of attraction rising inside her. He was so handsome it was hard not to be totally overwhelmed by him. That overpowering sensation was what scared her. She recognised the danger, that it would be all too easy to fall for this man.

'So, is this where you bring all your women?' She tried to lighten the mood between them, distance herself.

'You make it sound as if I have a harem.' He grinned. 'There haven't been that many women in my life.'

'I don't believe that.'

'It's true. I'm extremely choosy.' He smiled.

'And you've never come close to getting married?'

'I didn't say that. I did come close once...seems like another lifetime ago now.' For a moment his voice was reflective, sad.

'What happened?'

'It just wasn't meant to be.'

The waiter interrupted them with their coffee.

'How about you?' Frazer asked suddenly when they were left alone again. 'Have you ever thought of getting married again?'

She shook her head. 'I told you, some people aren't cut out for marriage, and I'm one of them.'

'Why?'

She shrugged. She didn't want to get onto this subject. 'Marriage just wasn't right for me.'

'Maybe he was just the wrong man,' Frazer said simply. 'How long have you been divorced?'

'Two years.'

'You don't strike me as a loner. You'll get married again, probably have about four children and be supremely happy.'

'I don't think so.' Her voice was carefully blank. But she could feel that ever-present knife inside her twist sharply.

'Tell me a little bit about living in California,' Frazer invited suddenly. 'What was it like?'

'California?' Her voice wasn't steady now. 'It was OK, I suppose.'

'Just OK?' He sounded disbelieving. 'It must have been more than that, surely? You were living with a film producer on a ranch. It must have been a very exciting lifestyle.'

'Not really.' Her voice was flat now. California had been the end of all hope as far as starting a family was concerned, and the end of her marriage.

'Why not?' he probed gently.

'It just wasn't, Frazer,' she told him softly. 'It's a time that I really just don't like talking about.'

'I kinda gathered that today, when you mentioned it. Is it because you don't like talking about Jon?'

'I don't mind talking about Jon. I just...I just don't like talking about my marriage break-up.' Her hand curled into a tight fist as it rested on the table, her fingers digging into her skin.

She hadn't realised she was so tense until Frazer reached across and took hold of her hand, opening it, running gentle fingers over the nail-marks in her skin. 'What happened, Emma? Was he a womaniser?' The tender concern in his voice made her heart thump fiercely against her chest.

The touch of his hand set her whole body alive with desire.

How easy it would be to lie and say yes. Adultery was a perfectly acceptable reason for a divorce. A better reason than her stark, bitter truth. But she couldn't lie to him. She looked into the darkness of his eyes and there was a part of her that yearned to tell him the truth. But she couldn't do that either. She couldn't admit to him, or to anyone, how raw and how incomplete she felt. Maybe if she told Frazer that desolate truth he would look at her differently; she would be less of a woman in his eyes. And his tone when he spoke of her ex-husband might soften towards sympathy. She couldn't bear it.

'We were just wrong for each other,' she said bleakly. She pulled her hand away from his; the touch of his skin against hers was too intensely disturbing. 'It's been a lovely evening, Frazer. But I think we should go now. It's getting late.'

'If that's what you want,' he agreed quietly. He put up his hand to catch the waiter's attention.

The bill was settled and then they walked towards the door. Frazer helped her on with her coat. She was wearing a black dress with delicate lacy straps and she felt acutely aware of his closeness, the way his fingers brushed accidentally against the bare softness of her shoulders as the dark cashmere coat was slipped into place.

'Thanks.' She turned and looked up at him. He didn't smile, and she wondered if her abrupt refusal to talk about her past had offended him. That was the last thing she wanted.

It was a wild night, the wind buffeting against the car as Frazer drove home slowly along the narrow country lanes. Emma tried to think of something to say, something light and impersonal, something that would take away the sharp feeling of tension that lay between them now.

'It was a lovely meal,' she ventured cautiously at last.

'I'm glad you enjoyed it.'

It was strange how they suddenly sounded like two polite strangers.

The bright headlights of the car sliced through the darkness. She watched the twists and turns of the road. The dark, gnarled shapes of the trees as they loomed in the glare of the headlights. She didn't want Frazer to be cool and aloof with her.

'I'm sorry if I sounded brusque when you asked me about my marriage,' she said quietly.

'It's OK, Emma, I understand.'

'Do you?'

'You're still in love with your husband.'

'No, Frazer, I'm not.' She looked across at him and wished she could see the expression on his face. The calm, deep velvet of his voice told her nothing. 'Really, I'm not.' Her voice was earnest. It was important to her that he believed her. He was so wrong.

'If you say so.'

'I do.'

Emma had just returned her attention to the road ahead when Frazer suddenly slammed on the brakes. Although she was wearing her seat belt she still would have jarred forward if he hadn't thrown a strong arm across her chest, pinning her to the seat.

The reason for their abrupt halt—a deer—stood poised in the middle of the road. It looked over at them enquiringly, as if to say, What are you doing on my road? Then daintily skipped away into the darkness of the night.

Emma let her breath out in a startled sigh of relief.

'Are you all right?' Frazer turned to look at her.

'Yes. It was lucky you weren't going fast.'

'Lucky for Bambi.' He smiled.

She was aware of his arm still across her. The coat she wore was unfastened, and the material of his jacket was pressing against the softness of her breast. The contact brought a sharp surge of desire welling up in her from out of nowhere. She felt the clamour of it inside, intense, absurd, but nevertheless very real.

'You're sure you're all right?' He pulled away from her.

'Yes, quite sure.' She couldn't look at him for fear he would see the need he had just summoned in her.

He reached and touched her face, turning it gently so that she met his eyes.

Emma could feel her heart drumming a rapid and uneven tattoo. The touch of his fingers sent a shiver of longing through her. For one wild moment she wanted him to pull the car further in to the side of the road and take her in his arms, explore her body, kiss her, touch her. The basic instincts that he aroused so thoroughly with just the slightest touch shocked her.

'You tremble when I touch you,' he observed quietly.

'I'm...I'm feeling a bit cold.' Never had a sentence been so far removed from the truth. Her body felt as if it was on fire.

Silently Frazer cursed the darkness of the car. He couldn't read the expression in her eyes. He thought he saw the invitation to kiss her, but he couldn't be sure. She gave out so many contradictory signals. He really wanted to take her into his arms, but his instincts told him that her emotions were fragile. Like the deer who had stood in the blazing glare of their headlights a few moments ago, she was poised for flight...

His hands returned to the wheel and he edged the vehicle forward again. Realistically he told himself that he had made the right decision. Emma was still in love with her ex-husband. Her vehement denial, the look of hurt in her eyes when she'd referred to her time with Jon, reinforced his conviction. He shouldn't get involved.

The gates to her property loomed up ahead.

Emma wondered if she should invite him in. She wanted to, but then there was another part of her that was urging caution. If her reaction simply to the brush of his arm was so vehement what would happen if he kissed her?

'I've really enjoyed the evening.' Her voice sounded false, as if it didn't belong to her.

'Yes, so have I.' The car rattled over the cattle-grids. Then he pulled to a standstill by her front door. 'I'll ring you about the arrangements for Saturday.'

'OK, thanks again, Frazer.' She reached for the doorhandle and hurriedly got out.

It was cold, and the wind tugged at her coat as she ran up to her front door. Aware that Frazer was politely waiting in the car until she was safely inside, she hurriedly searched through her handbag for her keys. She couldn't find them.

'Lost your keys?' Frazer climbed out of the car.

'No. They must be in here somewhere. It's just dark and I can't see properly. It's OK, you go on.'

He ignored her and followed her up to the door.

Feeling foolish, she rooted more frantically through the contents of her bag. She wanted him to leave...and quickly. But for no other reason than the fact that she wanted to invite him inside...wanted to get closer to him. Close enough to run her fingers through the darkness of his hair, press her lips again the firm sensual softness of his...

Her fingers closed with relief over the cold clasp of her keyring. 'Here they are. I won't detain you—'

'You're not detaining me.' He reached to take the keys from her hand. The gentle warmth of his skin against the coolness of hers made her quiver.

'You know, we're never going to pass as an engaged couple if you flinch every time I come near you.' His voice was quiet, barely audible over the rush of the wind in the trees.

'I didn't flinch.'

'Didn't you?'

'No.' She took a deep breath. 'I'm a little on edge—'

'A lot on edge,' he corrected. He smiled, a half-teasing, half-serious kind of smile. 'What's the matter? Are you frightened I might try to seduce you?'

'No, I am not!' She tried to sound indignant, but in fact she was more worried that he wouldn't have to try too hard.

'That's all right, then.'

Before she realised his intention he bent his head and kissed her.

The kiss was brief, but very intense, and it was so masterfully seductive that it swept all coherent thoughts out of her mind.

She felt breathless as he pulled away. 'Just getting into character for Saturday,' he assured her.

She watched as he put her key into the lock for her. 'Goodnight, Emma, sweet dreams,' he said softly before walking away.

She let herself into the house and then leaned back against the door.

'Just getting into character', he had said, his voice so nonchalant. Yet her lips still burnt from the sweetness of that kiss. Her body was on fire. Had she imagined the chemistry, the hedonistic bliss that had just occurred between them?

# CHAPTER SEVEN

EMMA parked her car on the main street in Glenmarrin and walked up towards the one and only boutique. The day was so grey that the sky seemed as if it was on the floor. The only brightness was the reddish gold foliage of the rowan trees that lined the street. Yet Emma felt as if the day was wonderful. A sparkle of pure happiness seemed to be glowing inside her. Nothing to do with the way Frazer had kissed her last night, she assured herself swiftly. One little kiss couldn't possibly have set so many tumultuous emotions racing through her body. That feeling of sensational arousal had been in her imagination.

'Morning.' The shop assistant smiled at her as she swung jauntily into the shop.

Emma smiled back and then spent an enjoyable few moments browsing along the rails. There was a surprisingly good selection of fashionable outfits.

The bell on the door sounded as someone else came in, but Emma was too engrossed in her shopping to look up.

She pulled a pale blue suit from the rail. It had a lovely straight skirt and a long-line jacket in a soft suede material. It would probably be perfect for the wedding. 'Excuse me?' Emma held up the outfit so that the sales assistant could see it. 'Do you have a hat that would go with this?'

There was an older woman standing at the counter, who turned to look round at her. 'Emma Sinclair?' she asked.

Emma nodded, wondering if she knew the woman from somewhere. She didn't look familiar, and Emma was sure if they had met she would remember her. She was in her early seventies, with a slim figure and long pure white hair which she wore in a French pleat. But it was her clothes that held the attention. She wore a flamboyant red hat and matching cape, a long grey pencil skirt and lace-up boots on her feet.

'Is that for the wedding?' the woman asked, looking at the outfit Emma held in her hand.

'Yes.' Emma wondered if the woman knew Ruth and Mark.

'So you're not planning a big white wedding, then?' There was disappointment in the frail voice.

'Oh!' Emma shook her head. 'It's not for my wedding. It's for someone else's wedding.'

'Thank heavens for that.'

Emma frowned. 'Do I know you—?'

'Ede McClarran.' The woman smiled. 'I believe that you are engaged to be married to my nephew?'

Emma suddenly wished that she could disappear down through the floor. 'Pleased to meet you,' she said in a slightly strained tone. Frazer was going to be horrified! What was it he had said? 'If Ede was in Glenmarrin we'd have serious problems.'

'I thought you were in Greece?'

'I was.' Ede grinned. 'But then my friend Jean Murray rang to tell me the news and I was so excited I got the first available flight home.'

Emma knew that the village of Glenmarrin had a strong gossip network, but that it had reached Greece in less than four days was astounding! 'And you've cut your holiday short because of me!' She was appalled. Her pretence had cost this poor woman an early flight home from her vacation.

'It wasn't really a holiday. I was attending a photographers' convention.' Ede waved her hand dismissively. 'It was too hot for me anyway. I expected it to be cooler at this time of the year.'

The shop assistant appeared from the back of the shop, carrying two hats. One was a very pretty blue, which she handed to Emma. The other was a large red creation with flowers on it. 'I'll just put it in a box for you, Ede,' she said.

'Yes, wrap it.' Ede smiled mischievously at Emma. 'I'd had it put to one side in case I made it back in time for Ruth's wedding. Now I'm wondering if I should save it for your big day and buy another one.'

Emma hoped she didn't look as disconcerted as she felt.

'Do you want to try on that suit?' the shop assistant asked her.

Before Emma could gather herself together to answer, Ede was taking charge. 'Just wrap it up for her, will you, Milly? And the hat. Charge it to Frazer. You know the address.'

The shop assistant nodded happily.

'No, really,' Emma protested. 'I need to try it on, and I insist on paying for it myself.'

'Nonsense.' Ede waved a hand dismissively. 'If you don't like it you can bring it back, can't she, Milly?'

Five minutes later, Emma emerged out onto the street with Ede, a new suit, a hat and a handbag! No amount of protesting had dissuaded Frazer's aunt from having her purchases charged to her nephew. She would just have to settle up with him herself, Emma thought dazedly.

'Now, you must come for tea,' Ede said happily as they set off down the street at a brisk pace. 'My car is just down here.'

'Well, I have my car, and I can't—'

'I'll drop you back at your car later,' Ede said firmly. 'I want to hear all about this whirlwind romance.' She stopped at a mustard-coloured Mini and opened the door to throw her shopping on the back seat. Then she took Emma's bags from her and tossed them in after her own. 'Off we go,' she said in a sing-song voice.

Emma felt as if she was being swept along by a tidal

wave, out of control and helpless. It was easier to just go with it.

Ede drove erratically. Emma clutched at her seat, thankful for the seat belt and the fact that Ede had assured her she didn't live far away.

'I can't tell you how pleased I was when I heard that Frazer had got engaged.' The gears protested loudly as she shifted them in order to go down a hill at a breakneck speed.

'I suppose he's told you that I've been trying to get him married off, or at least settled, for a while now?'

'Yes, he did.' Emma smiled.

'I shouldn't have interfered, but I was concerned when I heard that Samantha was coming home for Ruth's wedding.'

'Samantha?'

Ede rounded a corner into a driveway, narrowly missing the high gateposts, bringing the car to an abrupt standstill outside a redbrick Georgian house.

She turned off the engine and looked at Emma. 'He hasn't told you about Samantha?' The older woman's face was a picture of perplexity.

Emma shook her head.

'They were engaged to be married.'

'Oh.' Emma's voice was flat. Samantha must be the woman Frazer had been referring to last night. She remembered how sad he had sounded.

'It's an age ago now—nearly four years.' Ede's voice was filled with consternation. 'I shouldn't have said anything. It's typical of me; something's on my mind and I have to blurt it out.'

'It doesn't matter,' Emma said soothingly. 'Really, it doesn't.'

Ede smiled and her distress faded. 'Of course it doesn't. Judging by the speed of your engagement, obviously Frazer has fallen headlong in love with you.'

Before Emma could say anything, Ede was climbing out of the car and leading the way into the house. 'Della we're home,' she called as she slammed the front door behind them. 'Be a dear and bring us some tea.

'Della helps me around the house,' she explained to Emma as she led the way through to the drawing room. A fire blazed brightly in the fireplace and chintz chairs were drawn up invitingly. Silver-framed photographs lined the mantelpiece and filled some of the side-tables.

Emma put down her shopping bags and picked up a photograph from the centre of the mantelpiece. Two children standing on the banks of a loch in their swimming costumes grinned up at her.

'Frazer, aged ten,' Ede said as she came to stand next to her. 'And his sister, Helen.'

Emma looked at the photograph intently. Frazer was thin and gangling; an impish grin curved his lips and his eyes sparkled with devilment. His sister was much smaller. She had the same thick dark hair and a pretty face.

'They look happy there, don't they?' Ede reflected. 'You would never guess they had been through a major trauma.'

Emma looked over at the older woman questioningly.

'It was taken about nine months after their mother left.'

Emma looked back at the photograph.

'They had come to terms with it by then,' Ede sighed. 'But it was hard for them. I did my best, but really a maiden aunt is a poor substitute for a mother.'

The door opened and Ede's housekeeper bustled in with a tray of tea and some scones.

'Thank you, Della.' Frazer's aunt settled herself in one of the chairs and looked over at Emma.

The door closed behind the housekeeper and for a moment there was just silence in the room, except for the crackle of the fire.

There was so much she didn't know about Frazer, Emma thought. She felt such a fraud, standing here, talking to his aunt. She was a lovely woman and didn't deserve to be misled like this.

Emma opened her mouth, about to tell the truth.

'I hear you are Robert Daniels' daughter?' Ede commented before she could say anything.

Emma nodded.

'Your mother's family weren't originally from America, were they?'

'Yes!' Emma was taken aback. 'How do you know that?'

'I think I met her at a local garden fête.'

'And you remember her from all those years ago!' Emma knew that her mother had made one visit to Robert's home. She had spoken briefly about it a long time ago.

'Sometimes I remember things more clearly from years ago than I do from yesterday,' Ede laughed. She poured out their tea and handed Emma the delicate bone china cup and saucer. 'But I remember your mother because she was different; she stood out from the crowd. Robert had invited her up for a few days, during the summer recess from Oxford. She turned up at that garden fête looking like a movie star. I suppose I remember it so well because I had quite a conversation with her and it really annoyed Robert. He had told her not to speak to me, because of the feud between our families, but she had just ignored him. She was a person who made up her own mind about things, as I recall.'

Emma smiled at that. 'Yes, she was.' She hesitated before asking, 'What exactly was that feud about?'

'It started as a dispute over the boundary lines to their properties and it degenerated, as these things can do, into a bitter battle of stubborn hostility. But your mother and I paid no heed to it on that summer day long ago.'

Emma sat down in the chair opposite. 'It seems really strange to hear you talk about her.'

Ede's eyes twinkled with devilment. 'I remember thinking she was far too good for the likes of Robert Daniels.'

Emma laughed. 'Well, I don't know about that. I suppose some relationships are just not destined to be.'

'Exactly.' Ede sat forward, a solemn look on her face. 'Like Frazer and Samantha. Between you and me, Emma, that girl was nothing but a gold-digger. She accepted Frazer's proposal when she heard that he had inherited his father's estate. But as soon as she learnt that it was running at a loss, she broke things off. Went to live down in London. Frazer went after her, but she wouldn't come back, thank heavens.'

'As you say, some things just aren't meant to be.' Emma tried to keep her voice light.

There was the sound of a door slamming, then the door into the drawing room opened abruptly, bringing a cool draught of outside air.

Frazer strode purposefully in. He paused when he saw Emma in the chair opposite his aunt. He took in the cosy scene, the tea table, the shopping bags at their feet, and his eyebrows rose as he met Emma's blue gaze.

'Well, speak of the devil.' Ede grinned at her nephew.

'I hurried over as soon as I heard you were home.' Frazer went across and kissed his aunt on the cheek. 'Everything's all right isn't it? How come you're back from Greece so early?'

'You didn't think you could keep me away once I had heard your news, did you?' Ede looked up at him with affection.

'You've heard, then?' Frazer looked over at Emma, and his dark eyes were probing and intense.

'Jean told me on the phone.' Ede said. 'Would you like a cup of tea, Frazer?'

'No, I haven't really got time—'

'Oh, nonsense, do stay and have a drink.' Ede got up from her chair. 'I'll just ask Della to make us a fresh pot.' She picked up the tray and left the room.

Frazer sat in the chair she had just vacated and stared

over at Emma. 'What the hell have you told her?' he asked irately.

'Nothing.' Emma's heart thundered against her breast. 'I wanted to tell her the truth, except that I've hardly been able to get a word in edgeways.'

'Well, imagine coming here! Talk about digging a big hole and then jumping into it!'

'Don't blame me! She hijacked me in the dress shop. Have you tried saying no to her?' Emma hissed, then grinned suddenly. 'You didn't even want a cup of tea.'

Frazer raked a frustrated hand through his hair. 'Fair point. What a bloody mess.' He glanced at the shopping bags by her chair. 'What's in there?' he asked suspiciously. 'She hasn't been shopping for our wedding, has she?' His eyes were wide with the appalling thought. 'Hell, the way things are going I wouldn't be surprised if she has her whole outfit and the church booked!'

'No.' Emma murmured soothingly. 'She's only got her hat.'

Frazer glanced over at her sharply. Then, catching the amusement in her blue eyes, he found himself grinning back. 'What a damn mess,' he murmured again, but this time his voice was softer, less strained.

His eyes moved over her. She wore jeans and a white cashmere jumper. Her red-gold hair was loose and fell about her shoulders in gentle waves. She looked the picture of femininity, all soft curves with large, wide, inviting eyes. He remembered the softness of her lips against his and then wished he hadn't. It was too sensually provocative.

'I suppose we should tell her the truth when she comes back in,' Emma suggested gently. 'It doesn't seem fair to mislead her like this. She's so excited about the prospect of your wedding.'

He nodded. 'Yes, we must tell her,' he said firmly.

Ede bustled back into the room, carrying the tea tray.

'Della was busy so I did the honours,' she said as Frazer got up to help her.

'I've been thinking,' she said as she watched her nephew putting the tray down. 'You'll have to book St Andrew's in lots of time. You know how busy that church gets.'

'Aunt Ede, we've got something to tell you,' Frazer said gently as she settled herself back in her chair.

'You're not going to have a church wedding, are you?' Ede looked from one to the other of them. 'I knew it when I saw you buying that suit this morning, Emma.'

'No, Ede—'

'Oh, Frazer!' His aunt cut across him briskly. 'Please get married in the local church. It doesn't have to be a big ceremony—really, it doesn't.'

'Ede, will you please let me get a word in?' Frazer said firmly.

Ede looked at him with large reproachful eyes. 'I don't know what your father would have said. You're trying to break my heart, aren't you?'

'No, of course I'm not.' Frazer sat down on the arm of Emma's chair, the fire dying out in him.

Ede poured out the tea and handed it over to him. 'And you haven't bought Emma an engagement ring yet,' she continued briskly. 'It's terribly remiss of you.'

Frazer didn't reply. If the situation hadn't been so awkward Emma would have felt like smiling. She was willing to bet that this sweet old lady was the only person in the world who could scold Frazer and render him speechless.

'Would you like me to ring my jeweller friend Martin? Make an arrangement for you to take Emma down to his workshop?'

'No!' Frazer cut across her with decisive firmness.

'Oh, you are such a spoilsport, Frazer McClarran.' Ede glared at him. 'Emma, you are going to have to put your foot down and tell him exactly what you want. A big diamond ring and a nice church wedding. Tell him.'

The momentary amusement inside Emma died. It seemed that she was going to have to be the one to break the bad news. She felt a stab of deep remorse that she had been the cause of this. 'Well, Ede...' she started hesitantly.

'The thing is, Ede,' Frazer cut across her softly, 'we feel that things are happening a little too quickly.'

Emma looked up at him, startled.

'We weren't ready to even announce our engagement, and somehow it's got out. You know what this village is like.'

'Well...yes,' Ede said doubtfully.

'We're just going to let things develop at their own pace. We're not making any plans for our wedding day until we've had time and space to discuss all the options.'

Ede shrugged slender shoulders. 'I suppose you're being sensible,' she conceded tentatively. 'You haven't known each other that long.'

'Exactly.' Frazer sounded pleased. 'There's no point rushing these things. We've got all the time in the world.' He finished his tea and put the cup and saucer firmly down on the table. 'I've really got to get back to work,' he said briskly. 'Can I drop you anywhere, Emma?'

Emma nodded. 'My car is in town.'

Ede looked as if she was about to try and dissuade them from leaving, then thought better of it. 'How about coming for dinner next week?' she invited instead. 'Emma still hasn't updated me about how your romance started.'

'Hasn't she?' Frazer murmured. 'We'll get together after Ruth and Mark's wedding, how's that?'

'Well, I'm going to the wedding,' Ede said. 'I've already rung Ruth to tell her I'm back. So you can tell me all the details then, dear, can't you? In fact, why don't I pick you up and drive you to the church? Frazer will be going with Mark, as he's the best man.'

Emma smiled. 'I've got a better idea. Why don't I pick you up?'

'Well, if you're sure.' Ede hesitated. 'Are you staying overnight at the hotel? Ruth informed me that a lot of people are.'

'The reception is at the Traveller's Rest in town, isn't it?' Emma said, perplexed.

'Yes, that's right. I won't be staying overnight; there's no point. The village is only down the road and Jean will probably run me home. But a lot of people from out of town are staying. It will mean they can have a drink and relax without having to worry about driving.'

'I don't drink much anyway—'

'You two can come and stay here, if you'd like.' Ede cut across her gently. 'I'll make up the double bed in the front room.'

'No, there's no need for that!' Emma felt her skin growing very hot and she avoided looking at Frazer.

'I've already booked myself a room at the Traveller's, Ede,' Frazer intercepted swiftly. 'And I took the liberty of booking one for Emma as well. So we're organised, but thank you for the offer.'

'I see.' Ede frowned. 'Well, at least you're sensible not to be driving home along those mountain roads late at night.'

'We're very sensible,' Frazer agreed with a wry grin.

'Not sensible enough to accept the offer of a double bed, though,' Ede observed abruptly.

Frazer bent to kiss his aunt goodbye. 'Now don't you go embarrassing my fiancée,' he said with a laugh. 'You're a wicked woman, putting thoughts like that into our heads.'

Ede shook her head. 'Separate rooms, indeed. I don't know who you think you're kidding!'

'Have you really booked me a room at the hotel?' Emma asked as they drove away down the drive and Ede's figure faded from view.

'Yes. The party will probably go on until the early hours

of the morning, so I thought it might be best. I was going to ring you and tell you today.'

Emma was silent for a moment.

'If you don't want the room, it's no problem to cancel it,' he said swiftly.

'No, you're probably right. It will be better to stay over.' Emma shook her head. 'I was just thinking about your aunt. She made me feel so welcome. I feel terrible for deceiving her.'

'Yes. But you saw how she was working herself up,' Frazer said grimly. 'If I'd told her that we weren't really engaged I think she would have burst into tears. She was heading that way when she thought we were trying to tell her we weren't going to get married in church.'

Emma sighed. 'I feel wretched about this.'

'Well, look on the positive side. It's cheered her up no end,' Frazer said decisively. 'We'll let her settle down, get used to the idea that there will be no wedding in the foreseeable future, then we'll call it off. Tell her we made a mistake, didn't know each other well enough.'

'She's a lovely person,' Emma said quietly.

'Yes, drives like a lunatic, though,' Frazer said with a grin. 'You were right to offer to take her to the wedding.'

'You're not kidding,' Emma agreed.

The light of the afternoon was starting to fade. The village came into view, lights twinkling against the haze of a mackerel sky.

'Ede was telling me how she stepped into the breach after your parents separated,' Emma said casually.

'Yes, she was marvellous. More of a mother to Helen and me than my own mother ever was. She was always there for us, supported us through good days and bad. Even went to our school concerts.' Frazer grinned. 'And believe me, that was a labour of love.'

'Is your mother still alive?'

'Yes, she has remarried and lives in Florida.' Frazer

shrugged. 'I was angry with her for a long time for just walking out on us. But now, as I've grown older, I can understand it. She was very unhappy here. The climate didn't suit her, and she hated the isolation. You only get one life, so I suppose you shouldn't waste it by being unhappy.'

'I suppose not.' Emma was silent. She couldn't imagine any circumstances being bad enough to warrant walking out on your children. She had yearned for a baby so very much, yet Frazer's mother had given her family up with what sounded like comparative ease. Life could be very unfair sometimes.

'Are you OK?' Frazer slanted a probing look at her.

'Yes, fine.'

'It's just that you seem...I don't know, sad sometimes.'

His perception startled her. She rallied herself and smiled. 'If anyone is sad it should be you. Talking about such a hard period of your life.'

'I got through it. Kids are remarkably resilient, you know. And of course I had Ede to help.' He grinned at her. 'Trouble is, she doesn't know where to draw the line. It was one thing helping me emotionally when I was ten, but I'm thirty-three now, and she's still dabbling.'

Emma laughed. 'She admitted to me that she's been trying to marry you off.'

'She's been very trying.' Frazer shook his head in droll amusement.

'She's only got your best interests at heart.'

'I know. But she's also a born romantic,' Frazer drawled. 'She just can't help herself.'

'I think there's a bit more to it than that,' Emma said quietly. 'She knows your ex-fiancée is going to be at this wedding on Saturday and she's worried about how you'll feel when you see her again.'

'You two *have* been having a cosy chat.' Frazer spotted Emma's car and pulled his to a halt in front of it.

'Maybe if you reassured her that your feelings for... Samantha are well and truly in the past, she might relax her fixation for marrying you off,' Emma continued, trying to ignore the note of sarcasm that had been so clear in Frazer's tone.

'You think so?' Frazer laughed and shook his head. 'I sincerely doubt that.'

'It might be worth a try?' Emma suggested.

'Emma, will you stop with the Pollyanna routine?' Frazer said dryly. 'I don't need anyone to fix my life. It isn't broken.'

'I never said it was.'

'Good, so just leave it there, OK?'

'It's all right with me.'

'And don't look at me like that.'

'Like what?' Emma glared at him, her eyes shimmering a bright blue.

'Like I've just wounded you or something.'

'You haven't wounded me. You've told me to butt out of your life and you're entitled to tell me that.'

'Good.'

'Good.'

They glared at each other. Then Emma turned away to pick up her shopping bags from the floor. 'And by the way,' she murmured, 'I owe you for a wedding outfit, a hat and a handbag. The bill's going to your house.'

'Is it, now?' Frazer sounded amused.

'It wasn't my idea.' Emma looked back at him angrily. 'It was your aunt Ede's.'

'I'm sure it was.' Frazer grinned.

'I'll settle up with you as soon as the account comes in.'

'Emma.'

His voice stilled her as she made to open the car door. She looked back at him.

'Why are we arguing?' he asked softly.

She stared at him. Something about the way he was looking at her made her heart start to thump erratically and painfully against her chest.

'I don't know…' Emma's voice trailed off as she found herself wondering if perhaps she had been angry because she had felt a moment's jealousy for this unknown woman, the woman he had once wanted to marry. The knowledge appalled her. She couldn't be jealous. Frazer was a friend, nothing more, she had no right to feel possessive.

'No, neither do I.' He reached out and touched her face.

It was a gentle, brief caress, but it made Emma's blood race through her veins, her heart stand still.

Then he leaned closer and his lips met hers in a passionately sweet kiss.

For just a moment she was so stunned she didn't respond. Then she reached up and laced her fingers through the soft darkness of his hair, kissing him back.

Their bodies were suddenly pressed very close together in the small confines of the car. His hand moved to rest at her waist, then upwards over the soft cashmere jumper, stroking provocatively over the curves of her body in a way that set her senses on fire. The kiss became fevered, hard, hungry, demanding.

He was the one to pull back. They stared at each other in stunned silence.

Emma's breathing felt heavy, as if she had been running a race. Her emotions were in chaos. She hadn't imagined the chemistry between them when he had kissed her last night. The sensuality was explosive, compelling, totally overwhelming. No one had ever kissed her like that before.

'I'm sorry, Emma, I shouldn't have done that,' he said quietly, sitting back in his seat, putting his hands firmly on the steering wheel.

'No.' She didn't know what else to say.

She reached for the doorhandle of the car and stepped out onto the deserted pavement. Darkness had fallen, and with it a sharp frost which tingled against the heat of her skin.

Frazer sat and waited until she had climbed into her own car. Then he drove away with a speed that would have done his aunt Ede proud.

Why had he apologised for kissing her? she wondered. It wasn't as if either of them was married. It hadn't been a clandestine kiss.

Maybe he was frightened that she was going to take their makebelieve engagement seriously? Which was nonsense. She didn't want a serious relationship with anybody. Then again, she didn't want to make love with a man who treated the whole thing too lightly.

Perhaps, on reflection, Frazer had been right to pull back and apologise. The feelings that had sprung between them had been frighteningly compelling. For the first time in her life she knew what the phrase 'sexually compatible' meant.

Yes, Frazer had been right to pull back, she told herself firmly. Yet the knowledge did nothing to silence the storm of yearning his kiss had unleashed.

# CHAPTER EIGHT

THE bride wore white. She seemed to float down the aisle,
serenely beautiful, her eyes misty through the gossamer
veil.

The groom turned as she reached his side, a smile of
pride and happiness on his face.

The minister began the service.

'Dearly beloved, we are gathered together here in the
sight of God, to join together this Man and this Woman...'

For a while Emma's thoughts turned to her own wedding
day. A day not unlike this one. A crowded church, a white
dress, a handsome man. Hearts full of love and hope for
the future.

Her eyes rested on Frazer. He looked like the hero in a
period drama in his three-piece dark suit. The sunshine
slanted through the stained-glass windows giving his dark
hair a blue glow.

'...and therefore is not by any to be enterprised nor taken
in hand unadvisedly, lightly, or wantonly; but reverently,
and in the fear of God, duly considering the causes for
which Matrimony was ordained...

'First, it was ordained for the procreation of children, to
be brought up in the love and nurture of the Lord...'

Frazer turned and caught her eye; he smiled. She looked
away, down at the hymn book in front of her.

She wouldn't think about her own wedding, she told herself firmly. Wouldn't dwell on the reasons behind the fail-
ure of her marriage. The accusation in Jon's eyes. The feeling of hopelessness, the pain. She took a deep breath. That
was all behind her now.

The bells pealed merrily as Ruth and Mark stepped back

out of the church just a short while later, hand in hand, as man and wife.

St Andrew's was on the top of a small hill, overlooking the rolling green pastureland towards the sparkle of the sea, where the fishing boats sailed safely into the village harbour.

A peaceful church with a lychgate, it dated back hundreds of years, witness to good and bad times for the community over all those generations. There was a sense of continuity about the scene: the happy wedding, and beyond the graveyard, guarded by the mighty oak trees with their twisted branches giving testimony to the gales that frequently swept in from the ocean.

Today, however, it was a playful sea breeze which whipped across the fields and caught the bride's veil, billowing it out against the cold, clear blue sky. Everyone held onto their hats and tossed the colourful confetti with whoops of delight.

'It's a lovely church, isn't it?' Ede said quietly to Emma as she came to stand next to her while loading another film in her camera. 'I'll have a word with Reverend Peters, if you'd like, see what dates he's got left for next year?'

Emma shook her head and laughed. 'That's very kind of you, Ede, but we've put that on hold for a while.'

'Spoilsport.' Ede clicked her camera and captured Emma as she laughed again.

Frazer's eyes kept drifting over to Emma. He watched her chatting with his aunt. Then a few moments later he watched as she went across to congratulate the happy couple. She looked very elegant in the powder-blue suit. She wore a wide brimmed hat which shaded her face, complementing its delicate heart shape and the brilliance of her blue eyes. He could hardly concentrate on what people around him were saying for watching her.

Now Emma was laughing with the bride, looking totally at ease. She was always so warmly natural, he thought. At the moment she looked as if she hadn't a care in the world, yet when he had glanced at her in the church he had caught an unguarded momentary expression in her eyes that had struck him to the core, such sadness, regret.

He wandered across to stand next to her, in time to hear Ruth change the subject from her own wedding to their engagement. 'We're all so pleased for you both. Frazer is a wonderful man.'

'My ears are burning.' Frazer grinned.

'They should be burnt to a crisp the amount of talking people have done about you this last week,' Ruth laughed. 'You're a real dark horse, getting engaged without so much as a hint to any of your friends about your new relationship.'

Frazer slipped a reassuring arm around Emma's waist. 'I was too busy pursuing the woman of my dreams to tell you lot what was going on,' he said, his tone light-hearted, joking.

The possessive way Frazer had put that arm around her made Emma remember the way he had kissed her the last time they had met. Her heartbeats increased wildly. It would be very easy to like the feeling of closeness, to get carried away with the pretence of belonging, both to him and to this community.

The thought made her pull herself discreetly away from him as soon as Ruth's attention had wandered.

Frazer looked down at her. 'I like your outfit,' he said gently. 'You look beautiful.'

There was a gap in the crowds and they were left momentarily on their own.

'Thank you.' For some reason she couldn't meet his eye.

'Emma?' He reached out and touched her face, tipping it up towards his. 'You're not angry with me for the other day, are you?'

She knew instantly that he was referring to the way he had kissed her.

'No, of course not.' She stepped backwards, breaking the contact of his skin against hers. 'That was just…just a bit of fun.' She forced herself to smile very brightly. 'Maybe we both got a bit carried away with this engagement lark.'

'Maybe.' His eyes were incredibly dark as they rested suddenly on the softness of her lips.

They were interrupted by Mrs Murray. She looked totally different out of her supermarket overall, her plump figure encased in a smart tweed suit and with a jaunty hat placed at an angle on her head. 'I'm so pleased, dear, about the engagement,' she enthused. 'Have you got your ring yet?'

'No, Mrs Murray.' Emma smiled and waggled a naked left hand impulsively. 'As you can see, we're not really officially engaged at all.'

'That's just a formality,' Ede added as she joined them.

'Of course it is,' Jean Murray echoed.

Frazer met Emma's eyes, but he said nothing. There was nothing to say, Emma thought dryly. Because they were both deceiving these people. How they had got so deeply embroiled in this pretence she had no idea. One little white lie and here she was being congratulated by the townsfolk. Perhaps coming to this wedding today had been a bad idea.

The photographer was calling for Frazer so that he could take a few group photographs. With a grin he left them, just as Jean Murray started into a conversation about the best place to buy diamond rings.

The crowd began to disperse towards the reception.

'Shall we make our way, Ede?' Emma asked as Mrs Murray paused for breath.

Ede didn't reply. She seemed miles away in thought, her brow furrowed, her eyes narrowed in contemplation. Emma followed the direction of her gaze. She was watching Frazer. He was standing slightly apart from the main wedding group now, talking to one of the bridesmaids.

'Ede?'

'Yes, yes, we should go.' The older woman seemed to gather herself together. 'I'll go and tell Frazer.'

Emma watched as Ede went across to her nephew. Her eyes moved to the attractive bridesmaid he was talking to. There were four bridesmaids in all, but she was the oldest— probably about twenty-eight, Emma guessed. The long peach dress looked very sophisticated on her. Her long blonde hair was twisted up on top of her head and secured with fresh flowers.

'That's Samantha Fisher,' Jean Murray informed her.

'Yes,' Emma said as she watched the way the woman looked up at Frazer, put her hand on his arm and then reached to kiss his cheek with an ease and familiarity born from long years of knowing someone. 'Somehow I thought it was.'

Frazer turned to talk to Ede as she reached his side, and with a smile at the other woman he sauntered back over towards Emma. 'I'm going to drive you to the reception, Emma,' he said. 'You can leave your car in the car park here.'

'I don't mind driving—'

'I know, but you may as well come with me. There's no point in us both bringing cars. We can collect your car tomorrow morning.'

'OK.' Emma looked around for Ede, and saw her walking down the path with her friend Mrs Murray.

'Ede's going with Jean,' Frazer explained as they turned to follow them. 'Apparently they have a lot of catching up to do.' He grinned. 'Don't ask me how that is possible, when they're never off the phone to each other, but—' he shrugged '—that's what she told me.'

Jean Murray's car was disappearing out of the gates of the church car park as they reached it.

Emma smiled at Frazer. 'Is it my imagination or did they seem to be in a hurry?'

Frazer shrugged. 'Lord alone knows why. The bride and

groom will be a while yet; they're having a few more photographs taken outside the church.'

Emma stopped to take her overnight bag out of the back of her car, then Frazer led the way towards a shiny Range Rover.

Emma's eyebrows lifted. 'Where's your car?'

'This is my car.' Frazer put her bag on the back seat. 'It's been in the garage for a service, so I couldn't use it last night.' He opened the passenger door for her and watched as she hoisted herself up into the high seat, pulling her short skirt down as it suddenly rode too high up her legs. 'That old jalopy of mine is really only for work...this is for pleasure.'

She tried to ignore the gleam of amusement in his voice, knowing full well he had been looking at her legs as he said that.

The door closed on her and then he walked round to get behind the wheel.

'They got a good day for the wedding,' she said lightly. She was trying not to think about the way he had just looked at her, or what had happened last time they had been alone together in a car.

He started the engine and pulled out down the country lane.

'Yes, they have been lucky.'

Her eyes flicked out over the fields. Sitting so much higher gave a good view. She could see all the way down the hill towards the village, and smoke curling from the slate roofs into the blue of the sky.

'What were you thinking about today in the church when you looked so sad?' Frazer asked suddenly.

The question took her by surprise. 'I wasn't thinking about anything.'

'Liar,' he accused softly.

She shrugged, and her heart thumped uncomfortably against her chest. 'I suppose I was thinking back to my own wedding,' she admitted. 'Weddings are like that, aren't they? They make you think about your own relationships.'

'I suppose they do,' he agreed. 'Did you get married in church?'

'Yes, it was a big white wedding.' Emma was silent for a moment. 'I really thought we would live happily ever after. We only lasted four years.'

She looked over at him. 'Did the ceremony make you think about the way things could have been between you and your ex-fiancée?'

'You're trying to change the subject,' Frazer said with a smile.

'And you're avoiding my question,' she retorted.

He laughed.

'Samantha is very good-looking,' Emma remarked. 'Is she still single?'

'Yes, and enjoying her life in London.'

'Ede looked worried when she saw you talking to her in the churchyard today.'

Frazer shrugged. 'Maybe that's because Ede seems to have taken quite a shine to you.'

'Has she?'

'She thinks you are, and I quote, "A lovely, warm-hearted girl."' Frazer looked over at her. 'And I'm inclined to agree with her,' he said seriously.

Something in his tone made Emma's heart race against her breast. She smiled, feeling flustered, embarrassed. 'But she doesn't know the real me. I'm horribly bad-tempered sometimes.'

'Are you?' Frazer smiled.

'Especially first thing in the morning.'

'Well, I can't comment on that. I've never seen you first thing in the morning...more's the pity,' he drawled huskily. 'Of course we could rectify that. We could cancel the room I've booked for you tonight and you could share mine.'

Emma felt herself colouring a bright, vivid red. She

cursed herself for having such sensitive skin. Frazer was just teasing her. Wasn't he? She glanced across at him, suddenly unsure.

He pulled the car into the car park of the Traveller's Rest and switched off the engine. Then he turned to look at her.

'That's not a serious suggestion, is it?' She found her voice from somewhere.

He leaned closer. She could smell the fragrance of his cologne, see the gold flecks in the darkness of his eyes. Gently he touched his lips against hers. The feeling was tender, and then explosive as she started to kiss him back.

His lips slanted in a half-smile as he pulled away.

She felt disconcerted, completely at a loss.

'I just had to do that again to find out if it really was as incredible as I thought it was,' he said in a husky whisper.

He was too attractive, she thought with a tinge of panic as she looked over at him. It would be so easy to fall for a man like him. 'Frazer, I'm really flattered, but—'

He reached and put a gentle finger against her lips, hushing her. 'It's OK, don't say any more. I don't know what came over me.' His lips twisted in a self-deprecating grin. 'Well, actually I do know what came over me. Let's just forget it…hmm?'

She smiled.

But it was hard to forget the need he stirred so easily in her. Even the light touch of his finger against the softness of her lips turned her on. The idea of sharing a bed with Frazer McClarran made her body burn with a desire that totally blew her mind. She tried to tell herself that it was because she hadn't slept with anyone in a long time.

The last person to make love to her had been her husband, two years ago. Since then she had rejected all male advances. But she was a normal young woman with normal needs. Frazer was handsome; he was passionate. It was natural that she would be tempted, but she was right to turn him down. She knew herself well enough to know that casual sex wasn't something she could deal with.

The loud sound of a horn made them both look round. The bride and groom's car had just arrived with a flourish, and behind that the car carrying the bridesmaids.

'We'd better go inside,' Frazer said.

'Yes.'

But neither of them moved immediately. Frazer reached and touched her face with a gentle hand. 'So, we've ruled out the double bed, but that doesn't mean I can't kiss you again, does it?' he asked.

'No.' She felt herself swaying closer to him, craving the caress of his lips with a hunger that felt as if it could never be sated.

Despite the gentleness of his words, his kiss was firmly dominant, masterful. It made her stomach feel as if she was on a rollercoaster.

She was breathless when he pulled back.

'Now we really have to go,' he said with a grin. 'Otherwise they'll be making the speeches without me.'

Her legs felt as if they didn't belong to her as she climbed out of the car. She missed her step as she turned towards the hotel and Frazer put an arm around her waist. His touch set another chain of reactions in motion.

If she felt like this when he kissed her, when he just rested an arm around her, what would it feel like to lie next to him, have his hands move over the soft, naked curves of her body? Would he be as masterful in bed as he was at kissing?

She tried to close out the erotic images, the burning thoughts. The truth was they caused nothing but heartache.

They left their overnight bags at the reception desk for a porter to take to their rooms. Then they found their way through to the champagne reception.

The afternoon seemed to fly by after that. The function itself was a buffet held in a large marquee out on the back lawns of the hotel. Sparkling chandeliers were suspended from the ceiling and the flower displays that adorned the tables were spectacularly beautiful.

By the time the speeches had been made and the cake cut Emma felt as if she had known everyone all her life.

Frazer stayed attentively by her side, introducing her to his friends. His manner was courteous and light-hearted. Emma tried to tell herself that the emotions he had stirred up in her earlier were fleeting, that the attraction she felt for him wasn't really as fierce and intense as she had thought. Then his hand accidentally brushed against hers and she felt the overwhelming tug of desire once more. It was so all-consuming that it scared her.

Samantha came over to stand beside them and Frazer introduced them. She was even more beautiful than Emma had first thought. Her skin was perfect, the lashes that framed her green eyes were long and dark, and she had a sweet smile, which seemed to be slightly wistful when she looked at Frazer.

'I believe congratulations are in order,' she said softly.

Suddenly another emotion seemed to come into play inside Emma. She couldn't exactly say what it was; it just felt like a dull ache. She tried to push it firmly away, but it remained in the background, grumbling like some kind of persistent toothache.

'Well, it's not exactly official yet,' Emma said lightly as she noticed the girl looking at her left hand.

'So, you haven't set a date?'

'Heavens, no, we're not in any rush,' Frazer said lightly.

Angela, who owned the hotel, joined them in time to hear that remark, and said laughingly, 'That isn't what I've heard. According to Ede, your wedding is imminent—the next big event to hit Glenmarrin.'

'No, I think the next big event is firmly in your court,' Frazer said with easy humour.

Angela patted the large bump in front of her wryly.

'Maybe, although the way I feel this could be the never-ending pregnancy. Take my advice, Emma, no matter how much Frazer nags at you, don't rush into motherhood. It's very uncomfortable, not to mention ungainly.'

'It's only for a few months,' Frazer said with a laugh. 'And I'm sure when you hold your baby in your arms the feeling must be incredible. Well worth all the discomfort.'

'There speaks a true man,' Angela joked. 'I'd watch him, Emma. I bet now he's decided to take the marital plunge he'll be wanting the children to complete the package. Four, I'd say at a guess, and all boys, of course, to carry on the family farm.'

'I was thinking six, myself,' Frazer said, laughing.

Angela rolled her eyes. 'Run away quickly, Emma, that's my advice,' she teased.

Emma smiled politely. She was glad that the band chose that moment to strike up the music. It distracted everyone's attention and the bride and groom took to the dance floor for the first dance of the evening.

Frazer left Emma's side. She watched as he led Samantha onto the floor. It was the traditional start for a wedding, she told herself. The best man always danced with the chief bridesmaid.

They looked good together. Frazer so tall and handsome, Samantha willowy and just a few inches shorter than him. She was gazing up into his eyes, her whole attention focused on him.

She looked like a woman in love. The notion created another ripple of disturbance inside Emma. She tried to focus on what Angela was saying.

'So, Ede's wrong and there's no date set at the church?'

Emma shook her head. Across the crowded room she saw Ede, sitting with Jean Murray and a few other older women. They were deep in conversation—probably drawing up a wedding list for them, she thought guiltily.

She looked back towards Frazer, his arms resting lightly

around Samantha's waist. Despite Ede's antagonistic feelings for Samantha, she would probably be perfect for her nephew.

'Of course, every single woman in the village is pea-green with envy. They've all been after Frazer,' Angela said airily. 'He's the catch of the century. Despite the fact that he's been telling everyone for years that he is a confirmed bachelor, we've all known he was a family man at heart.'

'Yes, I think you're right,' Emma said quietly. And Samantha could probably bear him those six bouncing babies that he had been talking so light-heartedly about.

Why was she thinking things like this? Emma asked herself, turning her back on the dance floor. What was wrong with her? It was this phoney engagement. It had started off all kinds of strange emotions inside her. She'd have to pull herself together. She would have to tell these people the truth, that Frazer wasn't her fiancé, that it had just been a prank that had gone disastrously wrong.

'Your ex-husband arrived back this afternoon, by the way,' Angela continued, gaining Emma's full attention again. 'He's got a whole team of production staff with him, so the hotel is pretty busy.'

Emma's eyes widened. 'He said he might return early, but when I didn't hear from him I presumed he had decided to wait until Monday after all.'

'I was hoping that he wouldn't come until next week, because we're so busy with the wedding, but we've managed to accommodate most of his team. Ruth's invited them to come and join the party later. I hope this marquee is going to be big enough to hold everyone; she's already invited practically the whole village.'

The band struck up a faster tune, and more people flooded onto the floor. Frazer parted company from Samantha and made his way back towards Emma.

'I think I've just seen your ex-husband,' he said.

Emma followed his gaze and saw Jon making his way through the crowd, followed by his entourage. 'Apparently Ruth has invited them.'

'Why in the hell has she done that?' Frazer didn't sound pleased.

'Well, it's not every day we get a film crew in the village,' Angela said with a laugh. 'We're all pretty excited about it. We might be famous at last.'

Jon sauntered over to join them. He was wearing a light-coloured suit and a dark shirt. 'Hello, sweetheart, how are you?' he said, reaching to kiss Emma on the cheek.

'Surprised to see you.'

'I did tell you I might be back sooner than planned.' Jon smiled at Frazer. 'Have you met my location manager, Lesley?'

Frazer shook hands politely with the attractive brunette.

'Hello...' The woman practically purred the word as she looked up into Frazer's eyes. She was wearing a mannish-type trouser suit but had a white T-shirt top underneath which showed a very curvy figure.

'And the rest of my camera crew...' Jon continued to introduce Frazer.

Emma's eyes moved around the group of men behind her ex-husband. She knew most of them. For a moment she felt as if she had stepped back in time to the hundreds of parties she had attended with her ex-husband. It felt bizarre seeing these people here.

'Have you ever thought of auditioning for a part in the movies?' Lesley asked, fluttering her eyelashes at Frazer and putting a hand on his arm, as if staking some kind of claim. Emma felt like pulling the other woman off him physically. The strength of her annoyance startled her.

'Never in my wildest dreams,' Frazer answered dryly, disentangling himself abruptly. He looked over at Emma. 'Would you care to dance?' he asked politely.

Her heart seemed to accelerate as she looked up into the darkness of his eyes.

He smiled and held out his hand.

'Thanks,' she said as they made their way out onto the dance floor.

'What for?'

'Rescuing me away from that lot. It was like a blast from the past, seeing all Jon's old cronies again.'

Frazer grinned. 'I thought you'd rescued me. Jon's location manager is attractive, but I reckon she could eat me for dessert and still have room for another course.'

Emma laughed.

Frazer's eyes moved over her long hair, the soft peach of her skin.

Emma was suddenly intensely aware of the way he was looking at her. Although the band was playing a slow ballad, she tried to dance slightly apart from him.

'Your friends are so nice, Frazer. They've made me feel very much at home, and I was just thinking that…really we should tell them the truth…' she started hesitantly.

'The truth about what?'

'The engagement, of course.' She looked up at him, her eyes wide and earnest. 'You've been so kind, going along with my stupid pretence. I've landed you in a real mess.'

'Have you?' One eyebrow lifted. 'I was just starting to think that the situation might be working to my advantage.'

'You were?' She was stunned by this admission.

'Well, yes. Take my aunt Ede. I haven't seen her this happy in years—'

'Yes, but it's not really fair, is it? She's going to be devastated when we tell her it's all over.'

Frazer shrugged. '"Devastated" might be a bit dramatic. She'll be disappointed, but then she'll get over it and start with the matchmaking schemes again. She's a very determined lady.'

'Yes.' Emma had to agree with that.

'Then there's the land,' Frazer continued.

'Yes…' She was surprised that he was mentioning the land he'd wanted to rent now. Why it should surprise her, she didn't know. Frazer was a businessman; the reason he had agreed to go along with this charade in the first place had been a business reason. 'I got in touch with my solicitor yesterday to see about arranging it for you. But unfortunately he's away on holiday at the moment. So it will have to wait until he gets back.'

'Do we need a solicitor to arrange it?' He frowned.

'I think we should do it properly, don't you? Have a contract drawn up.'

'If you want.' He shrugged.

Someone jostled against her as they turned, and Frazer pulled her gently but firmly close in against him.

The effect on her senses was catastrophic. She was aware of everything about him: the tang of his aftershave, the hard, lean muscles of his body pressed against hers, his hand resting lightly against her waist.

For a while he didn't speak, then, as he bent his head to say something to her, his lips brushed against the side of her face. It might have been unintentional but it created a shivery, sensual feeling inside Emma that was deliciously erotic.

'Anyway, as I was saying. I'm not doing so badly out of our arrangement,' he murmured against her ear. 'Plus I get to monopolise the most beautiful woman in the room. Now that has to be the most perfect part of the agreement by far.'

'You were dancing with a beautiful woman a few moments ago, and probably saying something equally flattering to her.' She whispered the words unsteadily, trying to fight her feelings. 'I think you are a bit of a smooth talker when you want to be, Frazer McClarran.'

He laughed at that. 'No one has ever accused me of that before.'

'I don't believe you.' She turned her head and looked up at him. It was a mistake. As she met the darkness of his eyes she felt her defences crumble little by little.

'Believe it or not, it's the truth.'

It probably was, Emma thought dazedly. This man could seduce a woman just with his eyes.

'And as for Samantha, we discussed the weather, where Mark and Ruth are going on honeymoon and how she likes living in London—probably just about in that order.'

Why did she feel so relieved by that statement? It was none of her business. Emma closed her eyes and leaned her head against the soft material of his suit.

The band played another ballad and they continued to dance. Emma would have liked the evening to continue just like this; it was heaven being in his arms.

It was only when the music changed and the band struck up a faster tune that Emma moved regretfully away from Frazer.

'Shall we sit down?'

He smiled. 'Yes. I'll get us a drink.'

However, as they made their way from the floor someone caught hold of him, and Emma found herself at the edge of the dance floor alone.

Jon came over to stand next to her. 'Can I buy you a drink?' he asked gently.

She shook her head.

'Who is that?' he asked, following her gaze towards the woman that Frazer was now dancing with.

'Samantha Fisher. She used to be engaged to Frazer.' Emma didn't know why she'd told him that.

'She's quite something,' Jon drawled with approval.

Emma's nose wrinkled in censure at the way he'd referred to the other woman, but she had to agree that she was stunning.

She had changed out of the long bridesmaid's dress now, and was wearing a red dress that showed her slender figure and long legs to perfection. Her blonde hair was loose and fell almost to her waist. A lot of the men cast admiring glances at her as Frazer twirled her down the centre of the dance floor.

'Very energetic, aren't they?' Jon remarked.

Emma didn't reply.

'Why did they break up?'

'I don't know.'

'Who can fathom the workings of a woman's mind?' Jon muttered bleakly. 'I got my divorce papers through yesterday. I'm now officially divorced…again.'

Emma turned to look at him. 'I'm so sorry,' she said quietly, and her eyes moved with gentle concern over his face. 'How do you feel about it?'

'Like someone's ripped out my heart and stuck it on a stake in the village square for everyone to look at.' His lips twisted wryly. 'It was all over the paper yesterday. Gina sold her story.'

Emma winced in sympathy for him. 'Ouch!'

'Yeah, it's really got messy. I can't believe how mercenary Gina has become. All she seems to think about is money.' He sighed. 'She's not at all like you.'

'She's got a child to think about, Jon.'

'That's what really hurts,' he muttered. 'I'm going to lose Bethany.'

'You won't lose her. You're her father, and as long as you are there for her—'

'But how can I be there for her? You know what my job is like, Emma. It's impossible.' He shook his head. 'If I manage to get her for one weekend a month I'll be doing well…' His voice broke for a moment. 'Hell, Emma, you know how much I wanted a family, how much I longed for a baby.'

'Yes, I remember.' Emma's voice was raw for a moment.

'This divorce is going to kill me,' Jon said shakily.

'You'll survive,' Emma assured him.

'I'd survive better if I had you. I must have been the biggest fool alive to walk out on what we had together.'

'Stop it, Jon.' Emma took a step back.

'I'm sorry. I know you're engaged. But I can't help the way I feel Emma. I still love you, you know.'

Emma shook her head. 'I'm not even going to have this discussion with you, Jon,' she said firmly. 'I suggest that for the sake of your daughter you try and reach some kind of understanding with Gina, not me. Now, if you'll excuse me?'

She turned away. Suddenly she needed to get out of here, away from the crowds, the jollity and the music. She headed for the exit.

It was surprisingly cold outside the marquee. The night sky was clear and studded with stars. The hotel was lit up and the lights spilled across the lawn, but she didn't walk towards the light. On impulse she walked away from it. The garden was long, and separated from the open countryside by a gurgling stream.

Moonlight played over the water and Emma stood by the trees, looking down at the silvery torrent as it raced towards the sea. The music from the party was muffled down here, the babble of the stream soothing. She took deep breaths and tried to clear her head of the different emotions, the different snippets of conversation that kept running around inside her.

Frazer joking with Angela that he wanted six children. Jon telling her how much he had wanted his child.

She took a deep breath.

'Emma.' The quiet voice from behind her made her spin round.

'What are you doing out here?' Frazer asked gently.

'Just…getting some fresh air.' Her voice wavered slightly.

He came and stood next to her. 'It's a bit too fresh, don't you think?'

'It's cold, but it's OK.' She looked back towards the water.

'Ruth has just thrown her bouquet. Ede was looking for you; she wanted you to catch it.'

'Just as well I wasn't there,' Emma said wryly. 'I think you and I have endured enough speculation for one day.'

'Maybe enough for one lifetime,' Frazer agreed, with a smile in his voice. 'The latest piece of gossip is that Jean Murray's husband is taking bets that we'll be married before the end of the year. Apparently if you'd have caught that bouquet the odds would have been shortened considerably.'

Emma laughed. 'I hope that's a joke.'

'Yes.' He grinned. 'But it's nice to hear you laugh.'

She smiled.

'Are you going to come back to the party?' he asked. 'The coast is clear now. The bouquet is gone, and so is Ede. Jean Murray is driving her home.'

'I wasn't avoiding Ede, or the bouquet...'

'Just Jon?' Frazer's voice was matter-of-fact. 'I saw him talking to you. What was he saying?'

Emma didn't answer immediately.

'He's really able to upset you, isn't he?' Frazer murmured.

Emma looked up at him. 'No...'

She saw the disbelief in his eyes. What would he say if he knew that she had been more upset seeing *him* dancing with his ex-fiancée? she wondered suddenly. What would he say if she told him that she wasn't normally a jealous person but that when he looked at Samantha she burnt with the emotion? The knowledge that she had no right to feel like that made everything a hundred times worse.

She shivered, and he took off his jacket to drape it around her shoulders. Its warmth was welcome. 'That's the second time you've lent me your jacket.' She looked up at him. 'You are quite a gentleman, Frazer McClarran.'

'No, I'm not.' He tucked a stray strand of her hair back from her face. The gesture was tender. 'I've got ulterior motives.'

She looked into the darkness of his eyes and felt her heart starting to race against her chest.

Then, without thinking, she stood on tiptoe and reached to kiss him.

His arms stole under the jacket, curving around her waist, holding her close against his body.

His lips were hungry against hers. His jacket slipped to the ground. Suddenly she wasn't at all cold. She was burning up with the heat of the desire he kindled so easily within her.

His hands curved possessively over her breast, and his lips grazed over her cheek towards her ear. 'I want you, Emma. I want you now.'

'I want you too.' The words were tumbling from her lips without any conscious intervention from her mind. It was as if she was suspended in time, away from reality, in free-fall, and the only person who could save her was the man she was clinging to now with a very real, passionate need.

# CHAPTER NINE

THERE was no one behind the reception desk. Frazer took the key for her room from the pigeonhole and then, taking her hand, he led her up the stairs.

As she watched him turn the key in the door she felt she was watching a scene from someone else's life. She wasn't really doing this.

The door opened and he led her inside. She leaned back against it as it closed. The room was totally in darkness.

Neither of them made any attempt to turn on a light.

'Are you sure about this?' Frazer asked, his voice low.

'No.' She smiled. 'I'm not sure about anything.'

There was silence for a moment. All Emma could hear was the distant music from the wedding party and her own heartbeats. As her eyes became accustomed to the dark she could make out the powerful silhouette of his body. She couldn't see the expression on Frazer's face, but somehow that made it easier to throw away caution.

'The last man who made love to me was Jon.' Her heart thumped nervously against her chest. 'I thought I was sure about that.'

Moonlight slanted into the room from the window behind him. It caught her in the ghostly shimmer of its light. Frazer could see her clearly. Her skin looked very pale, her eyes very bright.

'The last thing I'd ever want to do is hurt you, Emma.'

'I know...' She closed her eyes. And Jon probably hadn't meant to hurt her. In a way she had believed him when he had said he still loved her, but sometimes love wasn't enough.

'If you want me to go, Emma, I will,' Frazer said quietly.

'I don't want you to go.' She whispered the words unsteadily. Her eyes flickered open. She wanted him to stay, chase away the loneliness, fill the emptiness inside her.

He reached out a hand and touched her face, just a whisper-soft caress with his fingertips across her cheek, but it stirred a million butterflies to life inside her.

He moved closer, his body blocking the light as his head bent towards hers. His lips soft, seductively seeking.

She met his kiss with bittersweet passion. She knew in her heart that this relationship couldn't lead anywhere, but she needed this closeness, needed his tenderness. Tomorrow could take care of itself. She wasn't going to think beyond the touch, the feel and the taste of now.

Slowly he started to unbutton the jacket of her suit. It fell to the floor. Then his hands moved under the silk of her camisole top, stroking the softness of her skin.

She felt the hot darts of wanton desire flood her body as he unfastened her bra. One by one her items of clothing fell to the floor. She felt her body pressed against the soft material of his suit as he picked her up and brought her to the bed.

'You're so beautiful,' he murmured.

She reached and trailed her fingers through the thick darkness of his hair. 'You're not so bad yourself,' she said, half laughing as she watched him unbuttoning his silk shirt. 'If you really want to know the truth, I've been admiring your body too.'

'Really?' He grinned, and kissed her on the lips in a lazy, seductive kiss that made her blood fire. 'I thought that was a man's prerogative.'

'Not at all.' Her voice was huskily uneven as she watched him unfastening the belt on his trousers.

She lay back against the feather pillows, a feeling of exhilaration in her stomach as he joined her, his skin satin-soft against hers.

'I knew the moment I first set eyes on you that you were going to be trouble,' he said with a smile.

'With a capital T.' She leaned forward and kissed him hungrily.

His hands moved over her, tracing the firm line of her breasts, the narrow gauge of her waist, the soft swell of her hips.

Suddenly they were both breathless, both out of control. His lips grazed over her in fervent kisses, acutely passionate, drugging her with sweetness. His hands teased her body. His body was hard against hers, powerful, playful. He made her giggle breathlessly as he nibbled against the softness of her neck and her ear, kissing her eyelids, then her lips in hot demand. Then, a moment later, he made her shiver with sweet need so serious it took her breath away.

She had known instinctively when he'd kissed her that he would be a fabulous lover, that the chemistry between them was perfect, but she was unprepared for how much he awakened her every sense. As if she had been sleeping until she met him. Frazer made her laugh at the same time as taking her breath away; he made her body tremble with need, arousing her to fever-pitch, then tormenting her playfully until she begged for him to continue.

Her hands moved over the taut muscles of his shoulders, and her nails rasped lightly over his skin as he took possession of her in a thoroughly dynamic, dominant way. Yet there was so much tenderness in his every movement, in his every kiss. She closed her eyes and savoured the sweetness, the desire exploding within her in spectacular rainbow colours.

She fell asleep cradled in the strong, protective circle of his arms.

When she opened her eyes the first light of dawn was creeping into the room. She was aware of a hand resting around her waist, fingers stroking softly up along the line of her spine.

Her dark lashes drifted upwards.

Frazer was lying beside her, propped up on one elbow, watching her.

She smiled sleepily, feeling wonderful as she looked into the darkness of his eyes. His hair was sexily dishevelled, his skin slightly darkened by early-morning stubble. The bedlinen lay low on his waist and hers. Yet she wasn't cold, and she wasn't self-conscious as his eyes moved over the curves of her body.

'Good morning.' He bent and kissed her lips. His skin brushed against the softness of hers abrasively, and the sensation was erotic.

'Good morning,' she breathed, her voice a throaty whisper. 'What time is it?'

'Very early.' He smiled and kissed the tip of her nose. 'I'm sorry, I woke you, and you were sleeping so deeply.'

'Yes...' She closed her eyes, savouring the relaxed feeling in her body. 'I haven't slept like that in a long time.'

'I should hope not.' His lips touched hers and she felt her breath catch as his fingers stroked over the firm lines of her body pulling her closer.

'You're not sorry for waking me at all.' She smiled.

'Guilty.' His hand moved to her breast, stroking her, stoking the fire alive inside her so easily. She moved beneath him, gently seeking his body like a flower instinctively moving towards the light of the sun.

It was only afterwards, when the searing heat of desire had been assuaged, that she thought about the responses her body had given to Frazer. They were unlike anything that she had shared with Jon, and yet she had loved her husband.

Her heart thumped painfully against her chest and she squeezed her eyes tightly shut, trying to close the thoughts out. But it was as if someone had just shone a great illuminating light down onto her. She was in love with Frazer McClarran. Over her head, out of her depth, crazily in love.

Even at the same time as her heart was telling her this in stark, no uncertain terms, her mind was wrestling with it.

She couldn't afford to fall in love with Frazer. Couldn't open herself up to a path which would only lead to heartbreak.

'Emma, sweetheart, are you OK?' he whispered against her ear.

She lay perfectly still, her heart thumping wildly against her breast, pretending to be asleep.

There was a part of her that wanted to just stay wrapped in his arms, cushioned from reality for as long as possible.

His breathing deepened as he fell asleep beside her. It was only then that she dared to open her eyes. She heard the first sounds of life outside, the melodious sound of the dawn chorus, then the hushed tones of people moving around in the hotel.

The bedroom was decorated in pretty shades of green and pink. Floral wallpaper and a fresh vase of lilies, waxy white against the deep green foliage, arranged in a glass vase on the bedside table. She lifted her head and looked at the clock on the bedside table. But all she saw was the packet of contraceptives that sat neatly next to the flowers.

They seemed to laugh at her, mocking her. She leaned her head back against the pillows, looking up at the ceiling.

Frazer had used contraceptives. At the time she hadn't even thought about it, her needs, her senses, too finely tuned in to the pleasure he'd been giving her.

Of course he was right to have used them. He was a mature, responsible male, sensitive, caring…and in today's world they were a necessary protection. She was sensible and mature as well. But even so the sight of those contraceptives made her want to cry. Frazer could never have made her pregnant. And because of that fact she was sensible enough to know that this was just a casual fling, that it could never be anything else.

'So, where do we go from here?' Frazer's deep voice

next to her made her realise that he had been watching her from the other side of the pillow.

She took a deep breath and put a smile very firmly in place. 'Down for breakfast. I'm starving.' She caught the momentary expression of surprise in the darkness of his eyes. Then he grinned.

'I'm starving as well, but breakfast wasn't the first thing on my agenda.'

Emma thought for a moment. 'In my experience, after a night of passion, breakfast is always the first thing on a man's mind.' The reply was deliberately casual. She swung away from him to sit on the side of the bed with her back to him.

'You talk as if you make a habit of waking up next to a different man every morning.'

She heard the laughter in his voice. 'No, of course I don't.' Her eyes flicked towards the door. Her clothes were strewn over the pale green carpet, testimony to their haste last night, and the total abandonment of her rational mind. She cringed, and felt a moment's anger with herself for being so weak.

Her eyes moved frantically around the room, looking for her overnight case. She wanted to pick it up and dash into the sanctuary of the *ensuite* bathroom. Put some clothes on, think sensibly about last night.

She located her small case beneath the windowseat. There was another case next to it. She frowned.

'Emma, why don't you come back to bed for a while?' Frazer's hand traced a whisper-soft caress down the long length of her back as he leant over towards her invitingly. 'It's still early—'

'Is that your case sitting next to mine?' she cut across him abruptly.

'I don't know.' He leaned forward to follow her gaze. 'Yes, it is.'

'What is it doing in here?' she demanded.

'I don't know. The porter must have made a mistake.' Frazer sounded unconcerned. 'I'm glad he did. It will save me having to walk back along the corridor in the suit I was wearing for the wedding.'

She turned her head to look at him. 'You did book two separate rooms for us, didn't you?'

'Yes, of course I did.' He leaned back against the pillows at his side of the bed.

Her eyes moved to the contraceptives on the bedside table and back to his face again. 'I don't believe you.'

His eyes narrowed on her flushed countenance, the glitter of fury in her expression. He didn't say anything. His calmness infuriated her further.

'You deliberately booked one room, didn't you? You cold-bloodedly set out to seduce me and I fell for it like a fool.'

Still he didn't say anything.

'I suppose you looked on it as another little advantage to our makebelieve engagement, did you?' Her voice trembled alarmingly.

'That's enough, Emma.' His voice was perfectly calm as he cut across her, so she was totally unprepared for the way he caught hold of her, bringing her back down into the bed with a strength that for a moment rendered her dumbstruck.

She found herself pinned gently, but deftly, against the softness of the covers as he sat over her.

'Let me go.' She glared at him fiercely.

'No.'

She tried to move away, but he held her easily.

'Now you've had your little say, I'll have mine.' He transferred her hands up above her head and held both of them in one strong hand. 'You may have a very delectable body.' His eyes raked over the firm tilt of her breast, the narrow waist with a look almost of disdain. 'But I can assure you that I'm not so hungry or desperate for it that I can't take no for an answer. I have never in my life had to resort to dishonest means in order to get a woman into bed, and I'm certainly not going to start with you.'

Her heart thumped painfully against her chest. As her temper started to abate she knew every word he was speaking was the truth. She also realised that her anger wasn't really with him; it was with herself.

'I don't know what the hell is going on in that mind of yours,' he murmured, 'but don't try rewriting history. What happened last night was a mutual flare of passion. You wanted me as much as I wanted you.' As if to illustrate the point he trailed one finger lightly up over her ribcage to graze almost carelessly over her breast. Immediately her body responded to his touch, hardening, aching for him.

Then abruptly he released her, moving away from her. He sat on the edge of the bed with his back to her.

Her eyes moved over the powerful contours of his shoulders.

'Frazer.' She whispered his name and he looked round at her. 'I was way out of line and I'm sorry.'

He didn't say anything, but the light in his eyes was gentle as he looked at her.

She reached out and took his hand in hers. 'I told you I was bad-tempered in the mornings.' She tried to make a joke of it.

His smile was fleeting. 'But there's more to it than that, isn't there Emma?' He pulled away from her hand and reached to touch her face, tipping it so that he could look deeply into her eyes.

If she had thought that a night of passion would still the urgency in her heart when he looked at her, when he so much as touched her gently, she had been mistaken.

She wanted him more than ever. But she had started something that couldn't possibly lead to anything serious. When a relationship reached 'serious', the subject of children started to slip into the equation. She had been through enough with Jon to realise that she couldn't go down that road again. That knowledge had struck terror into her heart this morning; it chilled her now.

'I guess I'm not so much of a modern girl as I like to think,' she murmured, pulling away from his hands. She lowered dark lashes over her eyes. 'It was easier to blame you for my own body's treacherous behaviour last night than it was to blame myself. But you're right, it was a mutual passion and I shouldn't have said what I did.'

'Treachery is rather a grave description of a night of passion, don't you think?' His voice was cool. 'Who did you feel you were betraying?'

'Myself.' She bit down on the softness of her lip. 'I've never been one for casual affairs, Frazer. Jon was the first man I'd ever slept with...the only man I've ever slept with. I thought when I married him that it was going to be for ever. That we'd have two children and live happily ever after. But life hasn't worked out like that.' Her voice was husky and uncertain. 'I feel like someone's thrown away my guidebook, and all the codes were in it for how I should live my life—'

'And now you're just floundering about, having meaningless flings?' he grated harshly. 'I'm sorry I made you feel so cheap.'

'You didn't make me feel cheap.' She watched as he got up from the bed, opened his case and started to dress. 'You're misunderstanding what I'm saying to you.'

'Am I?' He zipped his jeans and pulled on a rugby shirt. Then he threw his other clothes in the case and snapped it shut.

'Yes.' She held the sheet firmly across her body as she leaned forward, her eyes imploring him to understand. She wanted to tell him that, far from making her feel cheap, he made her feel more special, more cherished than she had ever felt before in her life. But she couldn't say the words. How could she say them? Where would it lead? They might continue with their relationship, sleep together, see each other every day, but then what? As soon as Frazer discovered that she couldn't have children he wouldn't want to make a commitment to her. It would be like being with Jon all over again.

'I was just scared, Frazer,' she said quietly. 'Sleeping with you was a big step as far as I'm concerned. I know it doesn't necessarily mean anything...but I just have difficulty getting with the modern programme. I need a new guide book for the twenty-first century.' She tried to make a joke, but it fell flat.

'I think you are more of a modern woman than you like to think.' Frazer looked over at her calmly. 'I didn't regard last night as a one-night stand, Emma. I thought it might be the beginning of something, not the end. You're the one who has been so quick to label it as casual.'

He watched the colour creep up under the pallor of her skin.

'Because I'm afraid to look on it as anything else.' Her voice was a mere whisper in the silence of the room.

He stood very still for a moment, and the raw anger seemed to die from his eyes. Then he came and sat down on the side of the bed. 'Why?' His voice was gentle.

She didn't answer him, couldn't answer him.

'Speak to me, Emma. I want to understand why you feel like that. Tell me what's going on in that heart of yours.'

She hesitated. Suddenly the temptation to do as he asked was very strong. There was a tenderness in his expression that made her long to bury her head against his chest. Tell him exactly why her marriage had broken down. Unload the pain, the burden of the knowledge that her inadequacies were to blame for Jon walking away.

He would probably be sympathetic, as Jon had been at first. But it hadn't really come as any surprise when the day had dawned on the fact that the problem was insurmountable. And from then it hadn't taken long for their relationship to crumble to dust. She couldn't go through that again, she thought fiercely. Not for Frazer, not for any-body.

'Are you scared because Jon was a womaniser?' Frazer prompted her lightly.

'Jon wasn't a womaniser,' Emma corrected him quickly. 'I told you that before. He wasn't even a bad husband.'

Frazer frowned. 'He left you, Emma! It hardly qualifies him for the Husband of the Year award.'

'Well, I wouldn't have got Wife of the Year either.' Her voice was bleak. There was no point telling Frazer the truth, because nothing he could do would make things better.

'OK, it takes two to make a bad marriage. But it's in the past, Emma, why can't you just let it go?'

Her heart thudded heavily against her chest. 'Because it's part of who I am.'

He stared at her steadily for a moment, then shook his head. 'I don't understand you.' He got up from the bed. 'But have it your way. Last night was a mistake. Let's just forget it, shall we?' He picked up his case and headed for the door. 'I'll see you downstairs later.'

'Damn!' Emma leaned her head back against the pillow as the door closed behind him. Somehow she had managed to make an almighty mess of things.

She stared up at the ceiling. But wasn't this what she'd wanted, she asked herself crossly. To keep Frazer at a dis-tance so that she wouldn't be hurt again? Wasn't that the plan?

'You don't want a serious relationship, Emma,' she told herself crossly. 'It will make you cry, make you unhappy. It will remind you of your imperfections.'

She remembered the way Frazer had held her so tenderly last night. He had made her feel incredible, wonderful. There was no better feeling in the world. She felt a jolt of utter desolation.

# CHAPTER TEN

THERE was hardly anyone in the dining room when Emma put her head tentatively around the door a little while later.

'Everyone's recovering from a hangover,' Angela said as she bustled into the room behind her. 'The party went on until five in the morning, I believe.' She waved her hand towards the tables. 'Take your pick and I'll bring you a pot of tea.'

Emma shook her head. 'I think I'll just pay my bill, Angela and get off. I've got work to do and—'

'Frazer has already paid the bill,' Angela cut in swiftly. 'I believe there was a mix-up with your luggage last night. I'm really sorry, Emma, I don't know how David could have made such a mistake. I told him quite clearly that Frazer had booked two separate rooms.'

Emma felt her skin blush with colour. 'It's OK.'

'Frazer wasn't too pleased.' Angela grimaced. 'He's gone for a shower. He said to tell you to go ahead and have breakfast; he won't be long.'

Emma felt as if she couldn't possibly eat anything. She just wanted to escape. But Angela was already leading the way across to a table in the window and it seemed churlish to refuse.

'Thanks, Angela, I'll just have a pot of tea,' she said as the woman passed her a menu.

She stared out of the window as she was left alone again. It was a bright morning; a clear blue sky beckoned. She probably wouldn't need Frazer to drive her to the church car park to get her car. She could walk from here. It was better to be independent. The more she was around Frazer, the more difficult it would be to keep a detachment from her feelings.

'Good morning.'

She looked up to see Jon standing next to her.

'Mind if I join you?' He pulled out one of the chairs opposite and sat down before she could answer.

'I'm sorry about last night, Emma,' he said immediately. 'I shouldn't have tried to dump all my problems on you. It wasn't fair.'

She shrugged. 'I'm sorry you're going through such a bad time,' she said honestly.

The first thing Frazer saw when he walked into the dining room was the way Emma was looking across at her ex-husband. The gentleness of her expression, the fragile glimmer of a smile in her wide blue eyes. His hands clenched and he had a momentary urge to drag Jon Sinclair out of that chair and punch him. How could Emma still love that man? He had walked away from her, had been the cause of the pain that sometimes was so clear in her eyes. Yet there was the softness of forgiveness in her voice when she spoke of him, and she jumped loyally to his defence at any suggestion of a criticism. Hell, she had even felt guilty of betraying him last night! That fact had been blatantly obvious when she had referred to their lovemaking as her body's 'treacherous behaviour'.

He raked a hand through his hair, irritated with himself for being so eaten up with jealousy. He had known the score before he took Emma to bed, had warned himself that she was still emotionally involved with her ex. But, along with all that sensible cautioning, he had hoped that she really wouldn't want Jon back. Looking at them now, sitting across the breakfast table from each other, he could only berate himself for being such a fool.

'Well, this looks cosy.' He stopped next to the table and forced a smile to his lips.

Emma looked up at him. She was wearing the same

white cashmere jumper she had worn when he saw her that day at his aunt's house. Sunlight was slanting over her, giving her hair a fiery gleam; her skin was very pale, her eyes shadowed as they met his.

'I'm just apologising to Emma for burdening her with my divorce problems last night,' Jon said casually. 'I really needed a sympathetic shoulder.'

'I'm sure Emma didn't mind at all,' Frazer said dryly. He pulled out a chair and sat down.

'Are we still on for dinner tomorrow night?' Jon asked suddenly, looking across at Emma again. 'I believe there's a wonderful restaurant out at—'

'Can we take a raincheck on that Jon?' Emma cut across him abruptly. 'To be honest, I'm feeling tired, and I've got a lot of work on at the farm.'

Jon looked disappointed, but he didn't try to dissuade her as he had the last time they'd talked about it. Frazer said nothing.

Jon shrugged. 'Is it OK if I bring the team out to your property this afternoon? I thought we'd make an early start at preparing the hall and the main reception room ready for filming. I've got a pretty tight schedule.'

Emma nodded. 'Come whenever you want.' She was really past caring, she thought wearily. She had thought that Jon's presence might upset her, but she was more churned up every time she met Frazer's dark eyes across the table than she was about anything Jon might say or do.

Angela brought the tea, and some toast. 'Can I get you men anything?'

'I'll have the full Scottish breakfast,' Jon said. 'And some coffee.'

Frazer shook his head. 'I'm going to get off in a minute, Angela. I've got to get back to work.'

'So I'm not the only one who has to work on a Sunday, then?' Jon said cheerfully.

Frazer ignored that. 'Would you like a lift back to your car, Emma?' he asked instead.

'No, thank you, Frazer. I'm going to walk.' She studiously avoided looking at him.

'See you later, then.' He pushed his chair back and left them.

'Everything all right with you two?' Jon asked curiously.

'Yes.' Emma poured herself a cup of tea.

'Come on, Emma, there was an atmosphere just now that you could cut with a knife. You've had an argument, haven't you?'

Emma's eyes met his across the table, clear blue seas of colour in a very pale face. 'That's none of your business.'

'No. But I care about you, Emma.' He was silent for a minute. 'You've told him you can't have children, I take it?'

She glared at him. 'Just because children were the most important thing in the world to you, Jon, it doesn't mean every man is the same.' Even as she said the words she was trying to convince herself of them, but they rang hollowly inside her.

'No, of course not.'

'Anyway, I haven't told him,' Emma murmured quietly. 'So don't you.'

Jon's eyebrows rose. 'I won't say a word.'

'Like you didn't say a word about my engagement?' Emma grated sardonically.

'I didn't say anything.' He looked discomfited. 'Well, all right, I mentioned it to Lesley when we were having morning coffee in here, and I think the waitress overheard me. But I didn't intentionally mean to let your secret out.'

'It was all over the village a few hours later.' Emma sighed. 'So just don't say anything else over coffee. This is my life, my business.'

'I think if you are going to marry Frazer McClarran then

you should tell him the truth, Emma. Children are a big issue, possibly the main one where marriage is concerned.'

'No, the main issue where marriage is concerned is love,' Emma said quietly, her heart thumping double time against her breast.

'But if you really believed that, you would already have told him the truth, wouldn't you?' Jon said quietly.

Emma sat silently. She didn't need to tell him because she wasn't going to marry him, she reminded herself fiercely. Frazer didn't love her. They had enjoyed a night together; she was the one who was blowing it out of all proportion. She was the one who had woken up this morning and had wished their engagement was for real.

'Anyway, I think, before you do tell him, there's something you should know,' Jon continued quietly.

Emma looked over at him and he hesitated.

'I was talking to his ex-girlfriend last night.'

'Were you?' Emma tried not to sound in the slightest bit interested.

'She seemed a bit upset that Frazer has got engaged.'

'He's a handsome man. Surely she didn't think that he'd just sit around waiting for her to come back when the mood struck her?' Emma's answer was sharper than she'd intended.

'Who knows?' Jon shrugged. 'She did tell me that she's staying around for a while. Her mother hasn't been too well, so she's taking unpaid leave from work to stay and look after her.'

'She sounds like a very nice person.' Emma sipped her tea. 'I don't wish to sound uncaring, Jon, but what has that to do with me?'

He shrugged. 'Nothing. It's just that she told me why she had broken off her engagement to Frazer in the first place…'

'Go on,' she prompted him as he hesitated again, all pretence at not being interested forgotten.

'Well, I'm only reading between the lines, here. But it sounded as if he wanted to start a family straight away and she wanted to concentrate on her career.'

'I don't believe you,' Emma said quietly.

Jon sat back in his chair, his eyes wide. 'What possible reason would I have to make a thing like that up?'

Emma crossed the street and put her shopping in the boot of her car. It was a bitterly cold day; the breeze that swept in from the sea felt as if it was coming straight from Siberia.

She would have given anything to go home and sit next to a blazing fire with a hot drink. Unfortunately her house was in chaos. Electrical wires were strewn over the ground floor, carpenters, electricians, actors, lighting technicians—a host of strangers, in fact, had taken possession, and it was about as much as she could do to get near the kettle in the kitchen.

Not that she had time to sit around drinking tea anyway. Two of her farm labourers hadn't turned in for work this week, and there was enough work waiting for her at the farm to keep her going until midnight every night.

She slammed the boot shut and got back into the car. Just as well that she was kept busy, she told herself. At least it stopped her from thinking about Frazer. It was two weeks since she had slept with him. Two long weeks and she hadn't had so much as a phone call from him. Not that she cared, she told herself angrily.

His aunt Ede had called up to the farm twice to see her. 'When are you and Frazer coming for dinner?' she had asked.

Emma had managed to put her off, saying that the house was in uproar and she had a mountain of work waiting for her around the farm.

The second time Ede had brought a cake and a batch of scones that she had baked. 'You're losing weight,' she had said severely. 'You're too thin to lose weight. And why hasn't that nephew of mine put a ring on your finger?'

Her concern had made Emma want to cry. Especially as it had come not long after Jon had informed her that he had seen Frazer at the hotel last night, having a drink with his ex-girlfriend.

'She looked gorgeous,' he had drawled. 'Her long blonde hair was drawn back with a black Alice band and she was wearing a stunning dress.'

Emma clashed through the gears as her car climbed the steep roads towards home. The information had galvanised her to send Frazer a cheque for the money she owed him, and a polite little note telling him that her solicitor was still on holiday, but that when he returned she would have some legal papers drawn up for him to rent the land he wanted. Then she had added a postscript, saying, 'Do you want to be the one to break off our phoney engagement, or shall I?'

Let him make what he wanted of that, she thought with some satisfaction as she pulled her car into the farmyard and parked next to the multitude of vehicles belonging to the film crew.

She carried her groceries into the kitchen. There was a crowd of people dressed in medieval garb sitting around her table, practising their lines. If she hadn't been so tired and fed up it might have been amusing.

Without taking off her coat, she put her shopping away and hurried straight out to the barn. She had a whole stack of grain that needed to be moved because the roof was leaking.

The sacks were incredibly heavy, but she struggled on. At least it was warming her up, she told herself positively.

'What on earth are you doing?' Frazer's harsh tone coming from behind her made her whirl around.

'Sunning myself in Barbados, of course.' From somewhere she summoned up the flippant reply. She tried not to notice how her heart raced with pleasure at the sight of him.

He was wearing a pair of jeans and a thick blue fleece top, but despite the casual appearance he looked incredibly handsome.

'What are you doing here, Frazer?' She turned away and picked up another of the sacks.

'I got your note and I thought maybe we should talk about it.'

'A phone call would have sufficed.' She tried to sound strong and together, but it was light years away from how she was feeling.

'Maybe.' He came and took the sack from her, dealing with it easily, as if it weighed nothing. Then he turned to face her. 'But I wanted to see you,' he said huskily.

Her heart felt as if it was turning over at those words.

'How are you, Emma?'

'I'm fine.' She hoped her voice sounded steady. His close proximity was having the usual effect on her. She wanted to tell him that she wasn't fine, that in fact she felt as if she was dying inside. The tender light in his eyes made her every emotion scream out against the unfairness of life. She loved him so much...wanted to throw herself into his arms and beg him to love her back.

She returned her attention to her work, trying very hard to clear her mind of everything except practicalities.

'Here, allow me.' He stepped across her and took the load from out of her hands. 'Why haven't you got one of your labourers to do this for you?'

'Brian was supposed to be doing it, but he's off sick.'

'Brian Robinson, I presume?' Frazer's voice was dry as he went across to move two sacks at a time now. 'I warned you about him; you should sack him.'

'I can't sack him! He's sick.' Emma was appalled. 'Look, I don't need your help, Frazer. I'm managing.'

'Yeah, so I see,' he said sardonically.

He moved the last of the grain, a task that would probably have taken her half an hour but had taken him a few moments. It was galling.

Then he turned to look at her, his eyes moving over her slender figure with a gentleness that made her emotions waver in the balance between defiance and desire.

She was wearing black trousers and a dark wool coat, but they did little to hide the gaunt lines of her body. 'Ede told me you weren't looking well,' he said softly. 'But I thought she was just...well, just pulling another one of her stunts to get me over here. I told her we'd fallen out, you see.'

'Have we?' Emma shrugged, and tried to look nonchalantly unconcerned.

'Come on, Emma, don't be awkward.'

She ignored that, and went to get a brush so that she could sweep up the grain that had spilt on the floor. 'What else did you tell Ede?'

'Nothing.'

Something about the expression in his voice made her stop what she was doing. Their eyes met.

Hell, he'd missed her, he thought fiercely. He'd tried to stay away, tried to give her some space, hoping she would sort her emotions out. But the effort was killing him.

Hidden beneath the gentle concern, Emma sensed the heat of sudden desire. She felt her heart pound painfully against her chest and wished he wouldn't look at her like that; it brought so many needs alive inside her. Feelings that she had been trying to deny for two weeks. He reached and took a piece of straw out of her red-gold hair. She probably looked a mess, she thought, remembering Jon's description of Samantha, when he'd seen her out with Frazer. How perfectly her hair had sat, how sophisticated she had looked.

'Anyway, as you can see, there's nothing wrong with me. I'm just a bit tired.' Emma stood back from him, her head held high. 'And, contrary to what you think, I'm managing the farm very well.'

'I'm sure you are, at a price. Namely your health. You look shattered, Emma. Look, let me help you. I'll send over a few of my staff and I'll sort out Brian for you—'

'I don't need your help.' She glared at him. 'And Brian doesn't need sorting out. He's ill.'

'He's in the bookies, Emma,' Frazer said wryly. 'He's well known for it. As soon as a cold snap comes along he takes himself off there and sits in the warmth, gambling his wages away.'

'He told me he'd got flu.' Emma frowned.

Frazer grinned. 'He thinks he's died and gone to heaven. He's got a woman boss. Not only does he think you'll never catch him out, because you're not likely to go into the bookies, but apparently he's laughing like crazy because you sent him home with an advance on next week's wages.'

'Well he told me his wife was sick and he was having difficulty paying the rent—'

'Emma.' Frazer cut across her briskly. 'Brian Robinson lives with his mother.'

Emma felt her cheeks flood with embarrassed colour. 'Well, I didn't know,' she said crossly. 'You told me that I had to watch him around the livestock. You didn't tell me that he was a compulsive liar.'

Frazer grinned, and the eyes that moved over her features were warm. 'I meant you just had to watch him, period. But don't feel too bad; he can be very plausible,' he said gently. 'And maybe you're right. I should have been more specific when I warned you about him. I'll sort him out for you.'

'Don't patronise me, Frazer.' She glared at him. She didn't want him to be kind to her, it made the ache inside for him worse. 'I'll sort Brian Robinson out by myself.'

Far from being annoyed, Frazer grinned. 'If that's what you want,' he said, but there was a note of respect in his tone. 'Meanwhile, how about coming and having some dinner with me tonight, over at my place?'

'I can't, Frazer. I've too much to do.' It took all her strength to refuse the invitation.

'Hey.' He reached and caught hold of her arm as she made to start tidying up again. 'You do realise that if you say no to me I'll be lynched by a little old lady, don't you?'

Emma looked up at him, and despite everything found herself smiling.

'Anyway, I meant it when I said we should talk.'

The new, serious note in his voice stilled her heart. 'What about?'

'About what happened between us the other night. Is there anything else?'

'It wasn't the other night, Frazer; it was almost two weeks ago.'

As soon as she'd said that she regretted it. She didn't want him to know that she had been counting every night, watching the phone, going into the village just on the off chance that she might catch a glimpse of him. 'Anyway, it didn't mean anything, so we don't have to talk about it, do we?'

'It meant something to me,' he answered quietly.

Her emotions were catapulted into turmoil as she looked up at him. 'That's why you stayed away, was it?' She tried to sound satirical, as if it really didn't matter. But she was fighting a losing battle.

'Yes.'

The quiet admission made her frown.

'You wanted me to stay away, Emma. It was in your eyes, in your voice.'

She remained silent, her heart beating double time against her chest. She couldn't deny what he was saying. Even now there was a part of her that wanted him to keep his distance, a part of her that was terrified of being hurt.

Yet there was a bigger part of her that was telling her to just throw caution away.

'Come with me now,' he said suddenly.

'I can't come now, Frazer. I've too much to do. And I'll want to shower and change before dinner.'

'OK, I'll collect you later.'

She shook her head, then found herself weakening. 'I'll drive over myself, later.'

# CHAPTER ELEVEN

EMMA lounged in the warmth of her bath and wondered what she should wear to go for dinner at Frazer's. Casual clothes, or something a little more upmarket.

She couldn't decide, and the water seemed to be cooling fast. She lifted her foot and turned on the hot tap with the side of her toe. Hot water gushed into the tub, then turned to a trickle, then stopped.

Emma frowned, sat up, and turned on the cold tap. Water gushed into the bath for a few minutes before also becoming a mere trickle.

'Now what's wrong?' Emma sighed. She got out of the tub and wrapped herself in a dressing gown. She wondered if the water problem was something to do with the film crew downstairs. They were still there, and would be working until late tonight in all probability.

She went out onto the landing and down the stairs, hoping to catch Jon so she could ask him. She heard his voice as she passed by the kitchen door. He was talking to a woman. Something made Emma pause.

'Frazer's not in love with her, you know,' the woman was saying knowledgeably. 'He'd do anything to get his hands on this property, and that includes marriage.'

Emma pushed the door wider. Samantha Fisher was sitting at her kitchen table, drinking coffee and talking to Jon. They both looked startled as they saw Emma standing in the open doorway.

'Oh, hi, we didn't hear you,' Samantha said with false brightness.

'Obviously,' Emma said dryly. 'I didn't realise I had a guest, Jon. You should have told me.'

'Samantha asked if she could pop in, see what life is like on a film set. You don't mind, do you?' he said easily.

Emma shrugged. 'No, I don't mind. But I don't care much for your choice of conversation.'

Both looked uncomfortable.

'There's something wrong with the water, Jon,' Emma continued briskly. 'Namely, there isn't any. Has someone done something to it?'

'Not to my knowledge.' Jon shook his head. 'I'll get someone to look at it for you.'

'Thanks.'

Without another word, Emma left them.

Emma returned to her bedroom and closed the door with a frown. Would Frazer do anything to get his hands on her land? The question troubled her for a minute, then she dismissed it. Frazer was perfectly happy to rent her land, she told herself firmly. Samantha was talking rubbish; perhaps it was jealousy. She pushed the whole thing from her mind and went to look in her wardrobe to decide what to wear.

The difference between her estate and Frazer's was starkly apparent as soon as she turned her car through his front gates.

The drive up to the house was tarmacked and lined with rhododendron bushes. The lawns and gardens were smoothly manicured.

She turned a corner and his house came into sight. A large, impressive building, with castle-like turrets at either side, outlined starkly against the clear moonlit sky.

Emma parked her car and felt suddenly nervous. Perhaps she shouldn't have come here. After all, what was there to talk about? How they were going to break the truth to Ede?

She stepped out into the frosty air and went up the front steps to ring the doorbell.

She was glad that she had chosen to wear a dress. This

house was so imposing. She would have felt distinctly underdressed in jeans.

The door swung open and the warmth of the house spilled over her.

'Hello, Emma, come on in out of the cold.' Frazer's welcoming voice made her relax instantly.

He looked incredibly attractive, in casual chinos and an open-necked cream shirt. Her heart thumped skittishly as he helped her to take her coat off, the slightest touch of his hand making her remember the pleasure he had given her on that never to be forgotten night at the hotel.

'Did you have any trouble finding the house?'

'No, none at all.'

They sounded like polite strangers, she thought. Only the way his eyes touched her body, noting the scooped neckline of her blue dress, gave the lie to their stilted exchange.

'Come through. I'll get you a drink.'

She followed him along the hallway.

The house was very opulent. It was obvious that money was no object. The polished wood floors were covered with exquisite Chinese rugs, the white lamps threw emphasis on paintings of the Scottish Highlands, crystal vases filled with fresh flowers were on every table.

Frazer led the way straight through to the kitchen. It was a cheerful room, with a red-tiled floor and wood cupboards—a country kitchen, with no pretension, warmed by the large Aga in the corner.

A plump woman, dressed in a black skirt and white blouse, her dark hair pulled back from a flushed face, turned to greet them. 'Dinner is nearly ready. I'd say another ten minutes.'

'Thank you, Rosa.' Frazer smiled. 'You haven't met, Emma, have you?'

Rosa smiled over at her. 'No, but Ede has spoken of you. I was really pleased to hear the news.'

Emma smiled, feeling uncomfortable. 'It's nice to meet

you, Rosa,' she said. A sheepdog sleeping next to the stove came across to welcome her with a friendly wag of his black tail. Emma bent to pat her, glad of the distraction. Behind her, tumbling out from the basket, were five black and white puppies, tails wagging enthusiastically.

'This is Bess and co,' Frazer said, bending to stroke the animal with affection.

'And that's Blaze,' he said with a laugh as one rotund puppy, completely black with just a white flash down its chest, jumped up to lick Emma's face.

'He's gorgeous,' Emma said, cuddling the little body close.

'A bundle of mischief, though.' Frazer straightened.

'Well, I'll get off, Frazer, if you're sure you can manage now?' the housekeeper said cheerfully.

'Yes, thank you, Rosa.'

'I thought you said you were cooking?' Emma asked as the door closed behind the woman.

He grinned. 'If I'd told you that you might not have come.'

'Can't you cook?'

'Yes, I can. But I'm not in Rosa's league. And anyway, I wanted to impress you. I was hoping she might be gone by the time you had arrived. Then I could have pretended it was all my own creation.'

Emma laughed. 'You wouldn't be so underhand, would you?'

'If it meant I scored some Brownie points with you, I would,' he assured her with a wry grin.

She tried not to be flattered. He was just being humorous, she told herself.

'What can I get you to drink?'

She smiled. 'A cup of tea would be wonderful. That's if we've got time before dinner?'

'Yes, no problem.'

Emma sat down in the easy chair next to the pine dresser.

The little black puppy tried to scramble up onto her knee. She picked him up and then he lay contentedly staring up at her with earnest brown eyes.

'You seem to have made a conquest,' Frazer said with a grin as he handed her a cup of tea a few moments later.

'He's a little dote.' Emma smiled.

'He's yours, if you'd like him.'

Emma looked up at him, startled.

'That day when you were trying to round up some sheep, I meant it when I said you needed a dog. Blaze has a good pedigree, and he'll be a faithful worker and friend for you.'

Frazer tickled Blaze behind one ear. He looked up at him adoringly, then closed his eyes with a little sigh, as if all was right with his world. 'I'll help you train him, if you want?'

Emma could feel his little heart beating against her, the warmth of his body was soothing. 'I'd love that,' she said earnestly. 'But I'll have to pay you for him. He's an expensive—'

'Emma, will you stop trying to pay me for things?' Frazer cut across her sharply. 'Blaze is a gift. There's no strings attached, no hidden agenda.' He straightened and moved away from her. 'And while we're on the subject, I've torn that cheque up that you sent me. I don't want your money.'

'But that was for my outfit for the wedding—'

'Yes, I know exactly what it was for. I don't want it.'

'But if you don't take it, that makes me feel…awkward.'

He slanted a wry glance at her. 'Why? Because we slept together and you feel compromised?'

'No.' She felt her skin flare with colour.

'I should hope not. Just let's forget the money, Emma. It's not important.' He went back to the Aga and started to serve up their meals.

Emma watched him quietly. She didn't know what to say to him. Part of her wanted to accept the gifts, but they scared her. Not for the reason he was espousing, but because she felt they drew her in deeper. She was in love with him. She wanted to lower all the barricades that she had been so carefully erecting. But she couldn't allow herself.

'That's about it. I think we should go through and eat,' Frazer said. He came across and lifted the sleeping puppy from Emma's knee. He didn't wake up, and Emma giggled as she watched how floppy his little body was as Frazer put him gently down into the basket with his brothers and sisters.

'He's had a hard day,' Frazer said with a grin as he stroked the animal gently.

'I know the feeling.' Emma stood up. 'I feel like flopping myself.'

'Well, there's a spare bed upstairs,' Frazer said quietly.

Emma felt her heart miss a beat as she met his eyes. He reached out and touched her face. The sensation was tenderly exquisite. 'No strings attached, of course,' he murmured.

She stepped back, her heart thundering wildly.

He smiled. 'Well, if I can't tempt you, I suppose we should go ahead and have dinner.'

Somehow Emma managed to rally her emotions enough to smile coolly.

The dining room was lit with the softness of a blazing fire and a few strategically placed lamps. They sat opposite each other, and for a while Emma determinedly kept the conversation light. The weather, the inconvenience of living with a film crew for two weeks. Farming. 'And now I've got no running water,' she told him. 'I don't know whether it's something the film crew have done or something more serious.'

'Ethan had problems with his water from time to time. I hate to tell you, but I think you'll probably find that you need to completely replace all the old lead piping on your land.'

Emma grimaced. 'Sounds expensive. This film crew might be damn inconvenient but it's a good thing I've got them.'

'So it's not so bad having Jon around, I take it?' Frazer reached and poured her a glass of red wine.

'Not as bad as I feared.' She shrugged. There was a moment's silence. 'Your girlfriend was at my house tonight. Having coffee with Jon.'

'Who's that?' Frazer asked, lifting one eyebrow.

'You know very well that I'm talking about Samantha.'

'It wasn't immediately obvious, as Samantha is more what I'd describe as an old flame.'

'I thought you might be getting back together,' Emma said casually.

'Why would you think that? When you're the one I took to bed.' He looked directly at her and she tried very hard not to blush.

'Will you stop talking about that?' she muttered uncomfortably.

'Why?'

'Because some things are of a delicate nature and shouldn't be brandished about.'

He seemed to find that remark amusing. 'I wasn't aware that I was brandishing it about.'

'Anyway,' she continued forcefully, 'I did think that you and Samantha might be getting together again. For one thing, Jon told me he saw you having a drink with her the other night.'

'You're not jealous, are you, Emma?' He asked softly.

'No, of course not.' She reached for her wine. If they were handing out Oscars for Best Actress, she should get one, she thought wryly. She was eaten alive with jealousy. 'Just because we spent a night together, I don't expect anything from you, Frazer. It doesn't entitle me to fidelity and undying love.'

'And this from the woman who told me she was old fashioned,' Frazer teased.

'Don't mock me, Frazer.' She glared at him. 'I'm trying to be mature about what happened between us.'

'You're not acting like a grown-up,' Frazer said casually. 'You're acting like a little girl lost in a fantasy world.'

'I beg your pardon?' She glared at him.

'You're still in love with your ex-husband. You feel guilty because you slept with me because you can't let go of the past. And you're hoping that by having Jon around and fluttering your eyelashes at him that he's going to magically become your knight in shining armour again.'

'That's just not true.' She stared at him in horror.

'No?' He looked at her with a raised eyebrow.

'No.'

'You want to wake up, Emma. Jon Sinclair is a waste of time. You're being incredibly naive if you believe for one minute that he's changed. I reckon the only person that guy is in love with is himself. You really made a mistake when you gave your heart to him.'

'And you'd know all about choosing wisely, I suppose?' she was stung to retort. 'I mean, Samantha is hardly Miss Honeyed Perfection, is she? Ede thinks she's a gold-digger, and that she only threw you over in the first place because your estate wasn't making enough of a profit at the time.'

Frazer shook his head. 'I love Ede, but she can be very cynical. Sam is certainly not a gold-digger; she's a warm and lovely person and I think a lot of her.'

Emma was unprepared for the way those words made her feel. It was as if someone had twisted a knife quite violently inside her. If Ede's version of why Frazer had split up with his girlfriend was wrong, was Jon's right?

With deliberate firmness she pushed those thoughts away. 'It might interest you to know that your paragon of virtue thinks you're only interested in me because of my land.'

'Does she?' His eyebrows rose.

'I think she's jealous. You know, if you play your cards right you might get her back.' The words felt as if they had been wrung from her.

'I don't think there is any chance of that. For one thing, she thinks I'm engaged.' Frazer frowned at her.

'Well, I'll make it right for you tomorrow.' Emma's heart thumped unsteadily against her chest. 'I'll go into the village and tell everyone that we made a mistake. How's that?'

Frazer met her eyes directly. 'Fine. Do it tomorrow.'

'I will.' Emma stared down at the plate of food in front of her.

The silence between them was overwhelming.

'Look, Emma, I don't want to argue with you,' Frazer said softly. 'I'm sorry if what I said hurt you. But I do think you should face facts, be more of a realist. It can save a lot of heartache.'

'I am a realist.' She looked over at him, and for a moment her mask slipped, her eyes shimmering with hurt.

He didn't know just how much of a realist she'd had to be. She would never have a child. Her marriage breakdown had been due to her own inadequacies. And since realising that she had fallen for Frazer she had faced reality squarely. She couldn't afford to fall in love ever again. Certainly a man like Frazer McClarran, who had never been married, had no children and was in his prime, was off limits. Frazer was the type who would want children. He would be good with them; he would dream of passing on his lands to them as his father had done before him.

'You don't know me, Frazer. So don't try to label me.'

She couldn't eat any more of her dinner, even though it was delicious. She glanced across at Frazer's plate and noticed he had finished his meal. 'I'll take these out for you,' she said, standing up and gathering up the dishes.

She put the plates by the sink in the kitchen, and for a moment stood looking out of the darkened window.

'You didn't eat very much,' Frazer said quietly from behind her.

She didn't answer him.

'You can't turn the clock back, Emma,' he went on as he came closer. 'If you were realistic you'd know that. If Samantha and I got back together it wouldn't be like it was before.'

'Why not?'

'Because of you, for a start.'

Emma turned to look at him, her heart beating painfully. 'I don't understand.'

'Don't you?' Frazer walked closer to her. 'Well, let me give you a hint.'

He bent closer and his lips touched hers, gently, sweetly. For just a second she trembled under his caress, trying very hard to make herself draw away. But her body refused the command.

She kissed him back, unable to help herself. The kiss deepened, became heated, hungry.

'How can you suggest that I get back with Samantha after what we shared together the other night?' Frazer asked huskily as he drew her into the warm circle of his arms, holding her against him.

Emma closed her eyes, savouring his closeness, her heart thundering against his chest.

Bess got out of her basket and came across to them, nudging them with her nose as if trying to get between them.

Frazer grinned down at the dog. 'Go away,' he said gently. But Bess wasn't about to be deterred.

'I think she's jealous.' Emma laughed shakily. She felt

glad of the interruption; it gave her a chance to try and gather her thoughts.

'I think you're right,' Frazer said, a teasing glint in his eye. 'But telling me that Samantha feels that way is total rubbish.'

Emma didn't agree, but she stayed silent.

'Let's go and relax in the other room.' Frazer took her by the hand and they walked through to the lounge.

It was a cosy room, with a roaring fire and a very comfortable-looking butter-gold settee onto which Frazer pulled her down beside him.

'Now, where were we before I was so rudely interrupted?'

'Frazer...'

Her words were silenced by his lips. He kissed her thoroughly, his mouth moving against hers with a seductive persuasion that was more powerful than Emma had ever known.

When she thought about his claims that she was still in love with her ex-husband she felt like laughing at how wrong he was. Nothing could ever be further from the truth.

He pulled back from her and looked into her eyes. For a long moment they didn't speak. The only sound was the crackle of the fire. It seemed to reflect the tinder-dry emotions inside Emma. There was a part of her that was so happy that he had pulled her into his arms and had held her like this, but the other...

She swallowed hard as he traced the outline of her lips with his finger. She wanted him to kiss her again. Touch her. She felt her body crying out for closer contact.

His hand moved to trace the outline of her breast through the satin material of her dress.

She felt her body answering him, a deep yearning ache starting to build inside her.

His fingers moved to the top button on her dress and his eyes met with hers. Questioningly.

She sat very still as slowly, one by one, he opened the buttons. She was wearing a delicate cream lace bra beneath. His hands held her underneath her ribcage and his thumbs reached to stroke over the fine lace with a firm touch of possession that made her gasp for breath.

'Tell me you don't love Jon Sinclair any more, Emma.' He reached to kiss her neck, whispering the words against her ear.

She closed her eyes, fighting for control over her treacherous body.

'Tell me you want me.'

Her heart slammed against her chest; she was sure that he could feel it hitting against his hand.

Her dress slipped further down, to lie around her waist. He pushed the lace of her bra to one side and his fingers closed in over the cool softness of her naked skin.

'Say, Make love to me, Frazer,' he murmured.

Her breath was catching in little shuddering jerks as she tried to switch off the need he had turned on so effortlessly. His head bent and his lips replaced his fingers.

She drew her breath in as the sharp sensation of ecstasy filled her mind so completely that she was no longer even able to try and think.

'I want you, Frazer,' she murmured softly, wrapping her arms around him.

He slid her further down on the settee and her dress was discarded. His hands moved over her stomach, stroking the flat lines and then tracing the outline of her pants.

Then he had moved her, and suddenly she found herself sitting on his knee. Her eyes opened wide and locked with his.

He held her hands in his and rocked her gently. 'This is reality, Emma,' he whispered. 'This need that fills us now.'

She couldn't say anything, could only gasp in pleasure as he pushed against her and kissed one rosy nipple.

Then suddenly he was pulling away from her. She

frowned and looked into his eyes. 'Why are you stopping?' Her voice was breathless and husky, and he smiled at the uninhibited need in her eyes.

Then he pulled her bra straight, so that it was covering her breasts, and reached for her dress.

'Frazer, what...what are you doing?' She was totally at a loss. How could he arouse her to this fever-pitch and then just stop?

'I want to ask you something.'

'What?' Her eyes seemed a deep shade of uncontrolled blue.

His hands rested on her hips. His touch made her wildly impatient. She needed him to continue. She wanted him.

She leaned closer to him and kissed him on the lips, softly persuasive. Her heart was in that kiss, and for a long while they just clung to each other.

'Make love to me,' she whispered as she pulled away.

His eyes moved over the fiery flame of her hair, the way her breasts rose and fell with the heaviness of her breathing, the softly pouting lips.

'Only if you will agree to marry me,' he said softly.

Stunned, she could only stare at him.

Then she pulled away. 'I can't marry you, Frazer.'

'Why not?'

She reached to take her dress from him, her fingers trembling as she slipped it on and tried to fasten the buttons.

'Because it wouldn't work.' She tried very hard to remain calm, but she couldn't meet his eye.

'Emma.' He stilled her hands, then tipped her face up to his with gentle fingers. 'Why wouldn't it work?' he asked softly.

'Because...' She swallowed hard. The touch of his hands made her tremble even more. Her mind seemed to be an incoherent jumble of fear.

'Because you've got a broken heart and a fetish for your ex-husband?' he finished for her. 'Is that the reason?'

'No.' Her heart thumped wildly against her chest. She pulled away from him and stood up.

'I told you that reality wasn't your strong point,' Frazer said gently.

Emma shook her head. 'That's just not true. It's two years since my divorce, Frazer. I'm over it.'

'In that case, put the past behind you, Emma, and look to the future.'

'I am looking towards the future.' Her eyes met his, a bright and vivid stare that was filled with determination. 'That's why I can't marry you.'

'I love you, Emma.' He said the words quietly.

Her heart contracted and turned over. She wanted to put her hands over her ears and close out his words. 'No...no, you don't.'

He stood up and reached to touch her. She backed away from him.

'You have feelings for me, Emma. I know you do. You couldn't kiss me the way you do, make love with me the way you do, if you didn't.'

She shook her head.

'Emma, do you honestly think that Jon is the right person for you? Can you really see yourself living with him again?'

'This has nothing to do with Jon.'

'So what has it to do with?' His voice hardened.

'It's to do with me. I don't want to get married again—ever, to anybody.'

'So what are you going to do? Live your life as a hermit because one man once hurt you? Run away from people who love you?'

Emma lifted her head defiantly and met his eyes, but her gaze was blurred with the shimmer of tears—so much so that she couldn't see him properly. 'Sometimes love isn't enough.'

'If love isn't enough then the world is a sorrowful place.'

'Well, maybe it is.' She turned away and ran a fierce, angry hand over her eyes to clear away the tears. 'I'll have to go.' She looked for her handbag. Then, remembering she had left it in the dining room, walked in that direction.

'You know you'll find it hard to manage that farm on your own.' Frazer followed her.

'I'll get by.'

'With the money from Jon, no doubt? How long do you think that's going to last? The place needs rewiring, new plumbing, a new roof, new heating, and you haven't even started on the outside.'

'I'll manage.' She found her bag and turned towards the front door. Frazer caught hold of her arm, swinging her round to face him.

'I want to help you, Emma. We'd be so good together. Won't you even consider my proposal?'

'I can't.' She bit down on her lip. 'I really can't, Frazer.'

He caught her as she swung away again.

'Give me one good reason why we couldn't be happy. Grow old together surrounded by our children and grand-children. At the end of the day, isn't that what life is all about?'

'For some people, maybe.' She pulled away from him. And then met his eyes. 'But not for me, Frazer. You see, I can't have children. That's the reason Jon left me in the first place.'

She saw the surprise in his eyes. Then he frowned.

'So you see, Frazer, I wouldn't be the type of wife that you would want at all.' She hadn't intended to tell him; he shouldn't have pressured her, she thought angrily.

'Problems like that can be overcome, Emma,' he said gently. He reached out and wiped a tear away from her face. Until that moment she hadn't even realised that she was crying.

'No, they can't.'

'There are all sorts of specialist treatments and doctors—'

'No.' Her voice came out much more vehemently than she'd intended. 'No, Frazer.' She softened her tone. 'I've been through all that with Jon. I'll never put myself through it again.'

He was silent.

'So you see, it's just as well that I turned down your proposal. Let's just forget that you ever made it, Frazer.'

She turned towards the door and left.

# CHAPTER TWELVE

EMMA turned the rearview mirror and studied her reflection. Despite the fact that she had spent time applying make-up this morning it did little to disguise the fact that she had been crying.

Her eyes were red, her skin slightly swollen. She sighed, and repositioned the mirror. She would just have to do, she thought, starting up the car engine.

She had an appointment at the solicitor's in the village to discuss the matter of renting off some of her property to Frazer. So, as much as she would have liked to hide herself away up here, it just wasn't possible.

It was raining heavily. It slanted across the car in wild, icy sheets, obliterating the scenery as she drove slowly down the mountain road.

'I love you, Emma.' Frazer's words from last night played over in her mind, just as they had all night. If things had been different how she would have been thrilled to hear those words, but now they made her feel so unhappy.

She had been right to say love wasn't enough. Frazer hadn't come after her when she had told him the truth. There had been a part of her that had hoped he would, that she would see his car behind her when she looked in the mirror.

But that was the naive side of her.

She parked her car in the village and waited to see if the rain would ease before stepping out.

Across the road she saw one of her employees, Brian Robinson, running into the turf accountant.

Emma frowned. Frazer had been right, it seemed. Brian wasn't ill. The rain eased a little, and she stepped out of the car. It was pointless even trying to put up an umbrella, the wind was so fierce. So she ran, head down, towards the doorway where Brian had disappeared a few moments ago.

It was warm inside, and it smelt of tobacco. Screens were displaying some race that was being run, and there was a lot of cheering and shouting from a group of men seated in one corner.

Brian Robinson was one of them. Without hesitation Emma walked over towards him. She saw the look of surprise on his face as he saw her.

'Brian, I take it you're feeling better now?'

'Oh, much better, Miss Sinclair, much better now.'

'Then may I suggest that if you want to keep your job you get yourself up to my property and get back to work?' Emma said calmly.

'Well, I'll just finish here and—'

'Now, Brian.' Emma's voice was uncompromising. 'And let me tell you that if this happens again I will not hesitate to sack you.'

Red in the face, the man got up.

Emma turned and walked out of the shop, aware that he was behind her.

The rain had stopped, but the streets were awash with water.

'I suppose you think that was funny, embarrassing me in front of my friends?' Brian demanded angrily from behind her.

'I suppose you think it was funny lying to me about being sick?' Emma turned and faced him squarely. 'I'll tell you this, Brian, if you think I'm a soft touch, you can think again. I meant what I said about firing you.'

'Well, good.' The man swayed, and she wondered suddenly if he had been drinking. 'I quit anyway. And let me tell you, Miss High and Mighty, everyone in the village is laughing at you.'

'Is that so?' Emma was calm. 'I think you had better go and sober up.'

'You think Mr McClarran is in love with you,' Brian sneered. 'All McClarran wants is your land. He couldn't give a damn about you.'

'Brian, I'm not interested in your—'

'Aren't you?' Brian laughed. 'Here's something that I think you'll find interesting. Frazer McClarran made a play for your cousin, Roberta, years ago. Just to get his hands on that land.'

'I suggest you go and have a black coffee, Brian.' Emma refused to be drawn.

'Ethan went mad. I've never seen him so livid. He went to his solicitor and changed his will. Told his daughter that if she didn't call things off with Frazer she wouldn't see a square acre of his land, that it would all go to you.'

It had started to rain again, but Brian seemed undeterred. 'But the real interesting thing was that the moment Ethan disinherited her Frazer McClarran was no longer interested. Dumped Roberta like yesterday's paper and took up with Samantha Fisher. She's the one he really loves. Trouble is, she hasn't got any land to go with those good looks.'

'I don't believe any of this,' Emma said impatiently. 'Go home, Brian.'

She walked away from him, her heart thumping unevenly against her chest. She couldn't believe that Frazer would be so mercenary that he would propose marriage just to gain more land.

'Well, if you don't believe me, go and look in the bar at the Traveller's Rest,' Brian called after her. 'Frazer McClarran and Samantha are in there together, sitting having a drink, looking into each other's eyes. Very romantic it is too.'

Emma glanced down the street towards the hotel. She wouldn't lower herself to go and look. It was none of her business anyway, she told herself fiercely. She had turned Frazer's proposal down. He could see who he wanted.

She glanced at her watch. She was early for her appointment at the solicitor, so she headed towards the supermarket to do some shopping first.

The shop was unusually crowded. Mrs Murray waved to her from behind the counter and continued the conversation she was having with two of her customers.

Emma picked up a basket and walked down the aisle. She only wanted bread and milk, but she lingered over making her purchases. Her eyes kept drifting out of the window, down towards the hotel.

She didn't really expect to see anything, therefore she was taken aback when, after a few moments, Frazer and Samantha walked out of the front door.

The rain was coming down heavily again, and they both ran along the street in the direction of a car. Samantha reached up and kissed Frazer quickly on the cheek before getting in and driving off.

Emma was unprepared for the anger that assailed her. She was livid, and at the same time enraged with herself for caring. It was none of her business, she told herself staunchly.

She dumped her purchases in her basket and went up to the counter to pay. At the same time Frazer entered the shop. Her eyes collided with his.

'Hello, Emma.' His voice was gentle.

'Hello.' She looked away.

He came to stand next to her at the counter. Emma was painfully aware of him, but she tried to pretend that she wasn't.

'Have you heard the good news?' Mrs Murray said cheerfully as she rang up Emma's purchases on the till. 'Angela has had her baby. A little boy.'

'That's lovely.' Emma smiled and took out her purse. 'Do you know what she's going to call him?'

'Robert William.' Jean Murray smiled. 'Angela is radiant, over the moon. And of course David thinks he's won the Lottery. A son. He came in here this morning, beaming all over his face, inviting everyone over for a celebratory drink.'

'They must be very happy,' Emma said quietly. Her anger with Frazer diminished under the greater ache of yearning.

'Well, I suppose it might be your turn next,' Mrs Murray continued happily. 'Are you two any nearer to setting a wedding date?'

There was a moment's awkward silence.

Emma took a deep breath. 'Frazer and I have decided to call off our engagement,' she said quietly. 'We made a mistake.'

Mrs Murray looked from one to the other in surprise. 'You've had a lovers' tiff,' she said.

'It's a bit more than that. We're totally unsuited.' Emma looked up at Frazer and then promptly wished she hadn't as all her emotions seemed to scream at her.

She noticed the way the raindrops glistened in the darkness of his hair, the dark warmth of his gaze on her lips. She found herself remembering the way he had kissed her last night, the tender way he had held her, told her he loved her.

He wasn't saying anything now, she told herself, angry with herself for recalling such things.

'Anyway...' She turned away and frantically scrabbled in her purse for her money, so she could pay and get out of here. 'Frazer is in love with his ex-girlfriend, aren't you, Frazer? You can't keep away from her, in fact.'

'That is just not true.' Frazer's quiet tone sent shivers of desire and anger simultaneously racing through her.

'Like hell it's not.' Her blue eyes shimmered brightly. She wanted to cry, she realised suddenly. She put her money down on the counter and, without waiting for her change, left the shop.

It was only when she was outside that she realised she had forgotten her purchases, but she couldn't go back.

'That was a good piece of acting.' Frazer caught up with her as she reached her car. 'I almost believed that you were jealous.'

'Did you?' She tried to sound as if she couldn't care less.

'I don't think you should have used Samantha as an excuse for us breaking up, though.'

Rain slanted its cold prickly fingers over Emma's face as she looked up at him. 'What would you have preferred me to say? That according to several people in the village you were only ever interested in getting hold of my land anyway? Or perhaps I should have just said that you'd changed your mind about me because I couldn't bear you children to inherit all this land that you care so passionately about?'

'I don't give a damn about your land.'

'Liar!' Her voice was unsteady. 'It was the reason you went along with our phoney engagement in the first place. And, according to Brian Robinson, it was the reason you made a play for my cousin, Roberta. Only Ethan foiled your attempts by threatening to disinherit her.'

'And Brian Robinson is a really credible character, isn't he?' Frazer drawled with derision. He held up his hands. 'OK, you've caught me out. I only care about getting that land. The argument over it has eaten away at your family and mine for years. Because of it, I went after Roberta. Because of it, I kissed you, made love to you and then proposed to you. But really, if that land wasn't so important to me, I would choose Samantha. She's my one real, true love.'

Emma flinched as if he had struck her.

'Happy?' he enquired bluntly.

'Why should that make me happy?' Her voice trembled. She wasn't sure now whether the wetness on her face was the rain or her tears.

'Because now you can run away from me with a real reason to hide behind. Now you can tell yourself that you hate me, that a marriage to me would have been a sham. And you can conveniently bury the real reasons why you turned down my proposal of marriage.'

She shook her head and made to turn away from him.

'That's it, Emma, run away,' he said mockingly.

She hesitated, and turned back to face him. 'You know why I turned down your proposal,' she said softly, her voice laboured by the painful thump of her heart.

'You were scared.' His voice became gentle now, and the eyes that moved over her face were tender. 'Your ex-husband hurt you, and you can't face going through that again.' He reached and touched her face, wiping the wetness away with the warmth of his hand. 'And ultimately you think that one day I will leave you because you can't have children.'

'You can't deny that it doesn't matter to you,' she whispered unsteadily.

'No, I can't deny that,' he said softly. 'But I meant it when I said I love you. I think that is enough to overcome any other problems.'

Emma shook her head. Desire and confusion clouded her mind, battling within her for supremacy. 'You just told me that Samantha was your one true love.'

'But you know that's a lie.' He bent and kissed her gently on the lips. The feeling was so exquisite, so heart-wrenching that she felt her whole body tighten with a bittersweet hunger. 'And that's the truth,' he murmured softly as he pulled away. 'That sweetness between us when we kiss.'

She couldn't answer him, couldn't think straight. The

heat of his lips was replaced by the cold air. The rain came down with a more persistent driving force.

'You're going to get pneumonia standing out here,' Frazer said now. 'Look, why don't we go into the Traveller's and dry off—?'

'Haven't you just come from there with Samantha?' The memory strengthened her with a return of anger.

'Yes, but—'

'Did you once date my cousin?' she asked him suddenly.

'Yes,' he answered her, quietly and directly.

'Why have you never told me that before?'

'It wasn't relevant. You haven't told me about all your ex-boyfriends—'

'She was my cousin, Frazer, I think it's relevant.' She reached and opened her car door.

'Fine, believe what you want.' Frazer's voice hardened behind her. 'Run away and pretend that you hate me.'

'I don't hate you.' Her breathing was hard and laboured in the tightness of her chest.

'But you don't love me.'

The softly spoken words made her swallow hard. She didn't look back at him, she couldn't. 'I think things are best left this way. Now you can chase after Samantha, have six bouncing babies and live happily ever after,' she said quietly. 'That is what you should do, Frazer. It's what I would do if I were you.'

'Thanks for the advice, Emma. I'll bear it in mind.'

There was a quiet finality about his voice that made her look back. She watched him walk away from her, his collar up against the rain. Then she got into her car.

For a while she just sat there, listening to the sound of the rain as it drummed down on the roof of her car. That sound seemed to fill her senses, cold and melancholy.

She closed her eyes and tried to compose herself. Did she really believe that Frazer was in love with Samantha Fisher? she asked herself quietly. The answer came back.

No. But he had once loved Samantha, and, given the right set of circumstances, it wasn't inconceivable that they might get back together.

Frazer had been right when he'd accused her of running away. But what else could she do? she asked herself helplessly. Frazer had admitted himself that he did care that she couldn't have children. If she followed her heart and accepted his proposal it would only be a matter of time before that dull need within him became a persistent ache. She knew all about the pain of that need. She lived with the reality of it.

'Damn you, Frazer McClarran,' she whispered. 'Damn you for making me fall in love with you, for starting this old hurt all over again.'

# CHAPTER THIRTEEN

'I'M SORRY I'm late, Mr Philips.' Emma sat down in the leather chair at the other side of the large desk.

'That's all right.' The solicitor pushed his glasses further up his nose and looked at her with concern. 'You're soaked through!'

'It's pouring down out there.' Emma shivered. She had been so upset when she was speaking to Frazer that she hadn't noticed how wet she was getting, and then she had almost forgotten her appointment here.

'Well, let's get things sorted out quickly and you can get home,' the solicitor said kindly. 'But first I'll ask my secretary to make you a hot drink.'

Emma accepted the offer gratefully. She was frozen.

'How are things at the farm?' Bob Philips asked as he got the relevant forms out from a filing cabinet. He was an elderly man, with thinning hair, but his eyes sparkled with lively intelligence, making him appear younger than his years.

'Fine…'

'Now, as you suggested on the phone this morning, I've drawn up a short-term lease for Mr McClarran.' He put the paperwork in front of her. 'If you'd like to look it over?'

'I'm sure it will be all right.' Emma's eyes flicked down over the printed page with very little interest.

'An interesting development, you renting land to Frazer McClarran.'

Emma looked up. 'Why do you say that?'

'Well, I'm sure you are aware of your late uncle's feelings where his neighbour was concerned?'

'Yes.' Emma hesitated. 'Is it true that Ethan changed his

will when he thought his daughter was…romantically interested in Frazer McClarran?'

'He thought about it.' Bob Philips sat back in his chair. 'He got me to draw up a new will, but before he signed it he had second thoughts.'

'He really disliked Frazer, didn't he?' Emma reflected.

'Ethan was a stubborn fellow. Lived in the past a lot. But I don't think he disliked Frazer. The feud over that land had gone back generations; his father and his father before him had argued with the McClarrans about it.' The solicitor shrugged. 'I reckon it had become a way of life.'

The secretary interrupted them, bringing Emma a cup of hot chocolate.

'Anyway, he saw the error of his ways over changing his will, and I think he was very glad afterwards that he did. Especially as it became blatantly obvious that Frazer cared deeply about his daughter. When Roberta was very ill, Frazer volunteered to be a bone marrow donor for her, but unfortunately he wasn't compatible when they ran the test.'

Emma's eyes widened.

'Nice man, Frazer McClarran,' Bob Philips commented. 'Of course, Ethan would never actually say he liked him; that would have gone against the grain. But I know he had a grudging kind of respect for him after his daughter's death.'

'There's good news and there's bad news,' Jon said when Emma walked into the kitchen.

'Give me the good news first,' Emma said, taking off her coat. 'I'm soaking and I'm cold and I could use it.'

'The water is fixed.'

'Thank heavens for that. I think I'll go and have a hot shower, see if I can warm myself up. What's the bad news?'

'According to the man who fixed the leak outside, your property needs completely new pipes.'

'Frazer has already told me that.' Emma shook her head. 'I dread to think how much it will cost.'

'Well, maybe this will help.' Jon handed her a cheque. 'It's for the amount we agreed, plus a bit more for the inconvenience you've had to endure.'

'It hasn't been too bad.' Emma looked at the piece of paper. 'Thanks, Jon. It will help.'

'We're just about finished. I think we'll be wrapped up here by dusk. Lesley is organising a drinks party at the Traveller's tonight, if you'd like to come and join us?'

Emma shook her head. 'I don't know if I'm up to it. But thanks for the offer.' She turned to go upstairs.

'If I don't see you tonight, I'll see you tomorrow before I leave. Oh, and someone called Ede has phoned you twice,' Jon called after her.

Emma cringed. She hoped sincerely that Jean Murray had not told Ede about their engagement being off. Emma went upstairs with a heavy feeling inside her. She'd have to return Ede's call and tell her the news herself, try and break it gently, if possible.

The prospect was not pleasant. She decided to have a shower first and wash her hair.

When she returned downstairs later the film crew had left. The house was strangely silent.

The crew had been working such long hours Emma had almost forgotten what it was like to be here alone. She picked her way through the debris they had left in the hallway and went to make herself a drink in the kitchen.

Rain lashed against the darkened windowpane and the wind screeched and rattled around the house as if someone was outside, trying to get in.

Emma stood at the sink, waiting for the kettle to boil, and tried not to think about her conversation with Frazer this morning.

'But I meant it when I said I love you. I think that is enough to overcome any other problems.'

She closed her eyes. She had been right to put a stop to their relationship, she told herself firmly. It could never work. She found herself remembering the day they had sat in the Traveller's Rest and Frazer had spoken about her cousin. What was it he had said? 'You look like your cousin. Roberta had the same colouring, the same way of holding a man's attention.' Maybe Frazer had never really been interested in her. Maybe he still held a flame for Roberta and she had merely rekindled those sentimental memories.

The sound of someone knocking on the front door startled her from her deliberations.

Hesitantly, she made her way through to the hallway. 'Who is it?' she called out.

'Your next-door neighbour.'

Frazer's amused tone set her emotions into chaos.

She opened the door and looked out into the wildness of the night.

'Ever had a feeling of *déjà vu*?' Frazer enquired wryly. 'I almost expected to see you in a long silver dress.'

'Molly hasn't been eating your underpants again, has she?' Emma rallied herself to make a joke, and stood back for him to step inside.

'No. But this little fellow is trying to eat my shirt.' Frazer parted the heavy overcoat he wore and she saw Blaze cradled beneath it, sheltered from the weather.

He gave a little yap and waggled his tail at Emma as Frazer came into the hallway.

'Here you are.' Frazer handed the wriggling warm body across to her as soon as she had closed the door. 'I brought you some food for him.' He put a white carrier bag down. 'And the shopping you forgot this morning is in there as well.'

'Thank you.'

There was a moment's silence. Emma stared up at him. Her heart felt as if it was going to burst it was thumping so heavily in her chest.

'I'm sorry about this morning,' she said quietly.

'Which part of this morning?' His lips slanted in a lopsided smile.

'Well…' She shrugged helplessly, trying so hard to keep practical thoughts in her head. The trouble was she kept noticing how handsome he looked, how his smile reflected in his eyes. How gentle his voice was. She found she very much wanted to go into his arms and be held.

She took a step back from him. 'Well, for a start, I don't really believe that you're just interested in my land.' She took a deep breath. 'You were right. I was looking for an excuse to run away—just as I was that morning when I woke up next to you at the hotel.'

Blaze nudged her with a wet nose and tried to lick her face. She put him down and he scampered around her feet, before dashing around the hallway to investigate.

'And I shouldn't have told Jean Murray that you're in love with Samantha. It was wrong of me. For one thing it's none of my business who you choose to see.'

'I'm not seeing Samantha,' Frazer said quietly. 'I was at the hotel to congratulate David on the birth of his son; Sam just happened to be there as well. Just as she happened to be there when I was having a quiet drink last week.'

Emma tried to look as if she wasn't interested. 'Well, as I said, it's none of my business.'

There was silence for a moment, and then Emma just had to blurt out, 'You're not attracted to me because I resemble Roberta, are you?'

He smiled at that. 'You are attractive, and you have the same colour hair, but that is where the resemblance ends.'

His voice was so easily nonchalant that she had no problem believing him. She felt her breath escaping in a sigh as some of the tension inside her started to subside. Not that it mattered, she told herself fiercely. She still couldn't accept Frazer's proposal. As if to prove that to herself, she said firmly, 'I hope you've told Ede that our so-called "engagement" is over. I'd hate to think she'd hear it from the gossips.'

'Jean has already been on the phone to Ede,' Frazer said.

'Oh, no!' Emma bit down on her lip.

Frazer shrugged. 'The first thing I did when I got home was phone her. But you know what this place is like. Jungle drums have nothing on Glenmarrin.'

'How did she take it?'

'In her stride. She thinks it's just a lovers' tiff and we'll make up.'

'Did you put her right?' Emma's voice was strained.

'In a fashion.'

'It's probably for the best, Frazer,' she said softly. 'I think maybe we both got a bit carried away by the pretence of being engaged. I mean…you once told me that you weren't really the marrying kind.'

He nodded. 'That's right, I did.'

He looked very serious now, the dark eyes intent on her face.

'So…so maybe we should go back to being just friends—go out together occasionally—'

'The trouble is, Emma, that it's very difficult to go backwards in a relationship. I think it reaches a point where it either moves forward or it doesn't go anywhere at all. We're at that crossing now.'

'I understand.' She swallowed hard. 'But I can't marry you, Frazer.'

'Because you can't have children?' He shook his head. 'There's a lot of people who can't have children, Emma. There's other things in life. Children aren't a main reason to get married.'

'They can be a main reason to get a divorce.'

The shrill whistle of the kettle interrupted them.

Emma turned away from him, glad of the diversion. She moved through to the other room. Her body felt as if it didn't belong to her; she felt coolly detached, as if she was in someone else's life, as if she was talking about someone else. Perhaps it was the only way she could cope with this, she thought dully. To detach herself from her emotions.

'Would you like a coffee before you go?' she asked, her back turned towards him.

'No. Do you love me, Emma?' Frazer asked her suddenly.

She turned the kettle off, and the piercing noise left a vast, uncomfortable silence.

She shook her head, but didn't turn to look at him.

'Do you love me, Emma?' Frazer asked again, his tone firm and uncompromising in the still of the room.

'It…it doesn't matter how I feel.'

'Like hell it doesn't.' He came and stood behind her, turning her round to face him with decisive hands. 'It matters to me.'

She couldn't look at him. Her heart was thundering in her chest. She felt like a scared, trapped animal, waiting for the kill. 'Please go, Frazer. I can't discuss this.'

He ignored her and placed a firm hand under her chin, tipping her face up to his. 'If you can tell me you don't love me, I'll go.'

She moistened her lips. Confusion darkened the blue of her eyes. 'You're not being fair, Frazer,' she whispered. 'Please, just go.'

'When you tell me how you feel, I'll go.'

'You know I love you.' Her voice was husky; tears sparkled in her eyes. She blinked them away, angry with herself. 'But I won't marry you.'

He smiled. 'I was thinking of a Christmas wedding. What do you think?'

'Frazer, you're not listening to me.'

'Yes, I am.' He bent his head and kissed her. The passion

that flared between them was instantaneous. She felt as if she wanted to melt into him. Never let go.

'I'm listening to your heart,' he said softly as he pulled back. He looked deeply into her eyes. 'I love you, Emma. I want to spend the rest of my life with you. I won't say that it doesn't matter that you can't have children, because I do want a family one day. But there are ways around that problem; we'll deal with it together.'

'But I can't deal with it. That's what I'm trying to tell you.' She pushed against his chest, but he didn't release her. 'Frazer, I can't go through the tests and the doctors again. It's like living life on some hideous rollercoaster—hope then despair, over and over, and with each new disappointment a little bit more of you dies inside. A little bit more of your marriage crumbles away.' She took a deep breath.

Frazer rubbed a gentle hand over her face, smoothing away the lone tear that trickled down the paleness of her skin.

'Then we'll adopt,' he said softly.

Her heart missed a beat and she looked up at him. 'You don't mean that, Frazer. It sounds great now, in theory. But in practice…' She shook her head. 'You'll want your own child.'

'But it will be my own child if we adopt.'

'You'll want the thrill that Angela and her husband experienced when their little boy was born. You'll feel as if I've cheated you.'

'I'd never feel like that.'

'You think you wouldn't now. But given time your feelings would change.'

'That's rubbish, Emma. I've thought very carefully about the situation since you told me. I've really searched my heart about it. And I can tell you categorically that I want you to be my wife. If I never have children that's God's will. If we can't adopt, then I'll live with it. But I can't live without you.'

Emma shook her head. 'I won't listen to this, Frazer, because you don't know what you're talking about. You don't know how you'll feel in, say, five years, when it suddenly dawns on you that you could have had a family but for me—'

'You are one hell of a stubborn woman, Emma,' he grated impatiently. 'I know you've been through hell, but you're forgetting one thing.' He tipped her face so that she was forced to meet his eyes. 'I'm not Jon. I'm nothing like Jon. I have nothing in common with the guy at all.'

'Haven't you?' Emma's heart pummelled so fiercely against her chest that she felt sure he would be able to feel it hitting against his body. 'Well, I heard that part of the reason you and Samantha ended your relationship was the fact that you wanted to try for a family straight away and she didn't.'

Frazer stared at her. 'Where the hell did you hear that?'

'Is it important where I heard it?'

'I suppose not, but it's not strictly the truth.' He released her and moved away. 'Yes, Samantha and I did start talking about the future, but she was the one to mention children. She was mapping out years like a military operation. She kept saying we should have a five-year plan.'

'It doesn't sound so unreasonable,' Emma said gently. 'If you don't make plans you can drift.'

'Yes.' He was silent for a moment, his back to her. 'But as soon as she started to talk about the future I realised something awful.'

Emma frowned. 'What?'

'I just didn't love her, Emma.' Frazer turned to look at her then. 'I'd drifted into the engagement after your cousin died. I was cut up, bereft about Roberta. I certainly wasn't thinking clearly.' He shook his head. 'I know it's no excuse. I hurt Samantha dreadfully, and I'm truly sorry about it. She is a lovely person, bright and beautiful and great fun.' He shook his head. 'But I didn't love her enough to want to spend the rest of my life with her.'

'I thought Samantha finished with you,' Emma said, surprised.

'I let people believe that.' Frazer shrugged. 'I felt it would ease the situation for her. She was feeling raw...''humiliated'', I think, was her exact word. In the event she took herself off to London.'

Frazer sighed. 'You can't imagine how guilty I felt. I went after her. I needed to know she was all right. I couldn't live with myself, thinking that I had driven her away from family and friends. I told her that everyone thought she was the one to break our engagement and that was how it would stay. But it was a mistake going down there. She thought I had changed my mind. It made her angry when I told her I genuinely cared about her but only as a friend.'

Emma remembered suddenly that day when they had sat in the lounge of the Traveller's Rest together and he had told her that delving around in the past could be a painful experience. She realised now what he had meant.

Frazer looked over at her clearly. 'So you see, children were nothing to do with our break-up. The conversation just brought my emotions into clearer focus.' He was quiet for a moment. 'I suppose that experience made me understand how easy it is to ricochet into a relationship without realising that your emotions are unreliable and that you're making a mistake. That's why I really tried to keep my distance from you. I thought you were still in love with your ex-husband, and I didn't want to be caught up in the crossfire.'

'I'm not in love with Jon.' Emma whispered the words unsteadily.

'No.' Frazer watched her steadily. 'You're in love with

me. We're going to get married, adopt six children and live happily ever after.'

Emma didn't say anything.

'You don't have to give birth to a child to be a loving parent, Emma,' Frazer said gently. 'Take it from me. My aunt Ede was a better mother to me than my own ever was. I love her more than words can say.'

'Oh, Frazer.' Emma glared at him reproachfully, and tears started to stream down her face.

'What? What did I say?' Frazer came across and took her into his arms tenderly.

She shook her head and buried her face against his chest. 'I was so determined, so positively sure until you said that…'

'Emma, sweetheart, I can't understand a word you are saying,' he said patiently.

'I'm saying we should tell your aunt Ede to dust off her hat. A Christmas wedding sounds like a wonderful idea.' She pulled away and looked into his eyes. 'I love you so much, Frazer.'

'I love you too.' He smiled. 'I think I fell for you the first time I saw you in that silver dress.'

He kissed her then, a slow, sensuous and wonderful kiss that made Emma's emotions smoulder with desire.

A series of short, impatient little barks made them pull apart. They looked over at the doorway. Blaze was sitting watching them, his head on one side.

'Blaze loves you too,' Frazer said with a laugh. He bent down and the puppy scampered across to them, delighted to be getting some attention.

At the same time the phone rang.

'That will be Ede,' Emma said with a smile. 'Do you want to tell her the happy news or shall I?'

*Harlequin truly does make any time special.... This year we are celebrating weddings in style!*

To help us celebrate, we want you to tell us how wearing the Harlequin wedding gown will make your wedding day special. As the grand prize, Harlequin will offer one lucky bride the chance to **"Walk Down the Aisle" in the Harlequin wedding gown!**

### There's more...

For her honeymoon, she and her groom will spend five nights at the **Hyatt Regency Maui.** As part of this five-night honeymoon at the hotel renowned for its romantic attractions, the couple will enjoy a candlelit dinner for two in Swan Court, a sunset sail on the hotel's catamaran, and duet spa treatments.

A HYATT RESORT AND SPA&reg;   **Maui • Molokai • Lanai**

To enter, please write, in, 250 words or less, how wearing the Harlequin wedding gown will make your wedding day special. The entry will be judged based on its emotionally compelling nature, its originality and creativity, and its sincerity. This contest is open to Canadian and U.S. residents only and to those who are 18 years of age and older. There is no purchase necessary to enter. Void where prohibited. See further contest rules attached. Please send your entry to:

### Walk Down the Aisle Contest

| In Canada | In U.S.A. |
|---|---|
| P.O. Box 637 | P.O. Box 9076 |
| Fort Erie, Ontario | 3010 Walden Ave. |
| L2A 5X3 | Buffalo, NY 14269-9076 |

You can also enter by visiting www.eHarlequin.com
*Win the Harlequin wedding gown and the vacation of a lifetime!*
The deadline for entries is October 1, 2001.

HARLEQUIN&reg;
*Makes any time special* &reg;

PHWDACONT1

# HARLEQUIN WALK DOWN THE AISLE TO MAUI CONTEST 1197
## OFFICIAL RULES
### NO PURCHASE NECESSARY TO ENTER

1. To enter, follow directions published in the offer to which you are responding. Contest begins April 2, 2001, and ends on October 1, 2001. Method of entry may vary. Mailed entries must be postmarked by October 1, 2001, and received by October 8, 2001.

2. Contest entry may be, at times, presented via the Internet, but will be restricted solely to residents of certain geographic areas that are disclosed on the Web site. To enter via the Internet, if permissible, access the Harlequin Web site (www.eHarlequin.com) and follow the directions displayed online. Online entries must be received by 11:59 p.m. E.S.T. on October 1, 2001.

   In lieu of submitting an entry online, enter by mail by hand-printing (or typing) on an 8½" x 11" plain piece of paper, your name, address (including zip code), Contest number/name and in 250 words or fewer, why winning a Harlequin wedding dress would make your wedding day special. Mail via first-class mail to: Harlequin Walk Down the Aisle Contest 1197, (in the U.S.) P.O. Box 9076, 3010 Walden Avenue, Buffalo, NY 14269-9076, (in Canada) P.O. Box 637, Fort Erie, Ontario L2A 5X3, Canada.

   Limit one entry per person, household address and e-mail address. Online and/or mailed entries received from persons residing in geographic areas in which Internet entry is not permissible will be disqualified.

3. Contests will be judged by a panel of members of the Harlequin editorial, marketing and public relations staff based on the following criteria:

   - Originality and Creativity—50%
   - Emotionally Compelling—25%
   - Sincerity—25%

   In the event of a tie, duplicate prizes will be awarded. Decisions of the judges are final.

4. All entries become the property of Torstar Corp. and will not be returned. No responsibility is assumed for lost, late, illegible, incomplete, inaccurate, nondelivered or misdirected mail or misdirected e-mail, for technical, hardware or software failures of any kind, lost or unavailable network connections, or failed, incomplete, garbled or delayed computer transmission or any human error which may occur in the receipt or processing of the entries in this Contest.

5. Contest open only to residents of the U.S. (except Puerto Rico) and Canada, who are 18 years of age or older, and is void wherever prohibited by law; all applicable laws and regulations apply. Any litigation within the Province of Quebec respecting the conduct or organization of a publicity contest may be submitted to the Régie des alcools, des courses et des jeux for a ruling. Any litigation respecting the awarding of a prize may be submitted to the Régie des alcools, des courses et des jeux only for the purpose of helping the parties reach a settlement. Employees and immediate family members of Torstar Corp. and D. L. Blair, Inc., their affiliates, subsidiaries and all other agencies, entities and persons connected with the use, marketing or conduct of this Contest are not eligible to enter. Taxes on prizes are the sole responsibility of winners. Acceptance of any prize offered constitutes permission to use winner's name, photograph or other likeness for the purposes of advertising, trade and promotion on behalf of Torstar Corp., its affiliates and subsidiaries without further compensation to the winner, unless prohibited by law.

6. Winners will be determined no later than November 15, 2001, and will be notified by mail. Winners will be required to sign and return an Affidavit of Eligibility form within 15 days after winner notification. Noncompliance within that time period may result in disqualification and an alternative winner may be selected. Winners of trip must execute a Release of Liability prior to ticketing and must possess required travel documents (e.g. passport, photo ID) where applicable. Trip must be completed by November 2002. No substitution of prize permitted by winner. Torstar Corp. and D. L. Blair, Inc., their parents, affiliates, and subsidiaries are not responsible for errors in printing or electronic presentation of Contest, entries and/or game pieces. In the event of printing or other errors which may result in unintended prize values or duplication of prizes, all affected game pieces or entries shall be null and void. If for any reason the Internet portion of the Contest is not capable of running as planned, including infection by computer virus, bugs, tampering, unauthorized intervention, fraud, technical failures, or any other causes beyond the control of Torstar Corp. which corrupt or affect the administration, secrecy, fairness, integrity or proper conduct of the Contest, Torstar Corp. reserves the right, at its sole discretion, to disqualify any individual who tampers with the entry process and to cancel, terminate, modify or suspend the Contest or the Internet portion thereof. In the event of a dispute regarding an online entry, the entry will be deemed submitted by the authorized holder of the e-mail account submitted at the time of entry. Authorized account holder is defined as the natural person who is assigned to an e-mail address by an Internet access provider, online service provider or other organization that is responsible for arranging e-mail address for the domain associated with the submitted e-mail address. **Purchase or acceptance of a product offer does not improve your chances of winning.**

7. Prizes: (1) Grand Prize—A Harlequin wedding dress (approximate retail value: $3,500) and a 5-night/6-day honeymoon trip to Maui, HI, including round-trip air transportation provided by Maui Visitors Bureau from Los Angeles International Airport (winner is responsible for transportation to and from Los Angeles International Airport) and a Harlequin Romance Package, including hotel accomodations (double occupancy) at the Hyatt Regency Maui Resort and Spa, dinner for (2) two at Swan Court, a sunset sail on Kiele V and a spa treatment for the winner (approximate retail value: $4,000); (5) Five runner-ups consist of a $1000 gift certificate to selected retail outlets to be determined by Sponsor (retail value $1000 ea.). Prizes consist of only those items listed as part of the prize. Limit one prize per person. All prizes are valued in U.S. currency.

8. For a list of winners (available after December 17, 2001) send a self-addressed, stamped envelope to: Harlequin Walk Down the Aisle Contest 1197 Winners, P.O. Box 4200 Blair, NE 68009-4200 or you may access the www.eHarlequin.com Web site through January 15, 2002.

Contest sponsored by Torstar Corp., P.O. Box 9042, Buffalo, NY 14269-9042, U.S.A.

PHWDACONT2

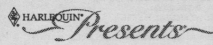

Brimming with passion and sensuality,
this collection offers two full-length
Harlequin Temptation novels.

*Full Bloom*

by *New York Times* bestselling author

# JAYNE
## —ANN—
# KRENTZ

Emily Ravenscroft has had enough! It's time she took her life back,
out of the hands of her domineering family and Jacob Stone, the
troubleshooter they've always employed to get her out of hot water.
The new Emily—vibrant and willful—doesn't need Jacob to rescue
her. She needs him to love her, against all odds.

### And

*Compromising Positions*

a brand-new story from bestselling author

# VICKY LEWIS
# THOMPSON

Look for it on sale September 2001.